"If You [...] Guarantee That I'll Be A Gentleman For Much Longer."

Realizing that she had been moving her fingers over his pectoral muscles and the upper part of his abdomen, she stopped immediately. "I'm sorry. I didn't realize…"

When she started to pull her hand away, he covered it with his and held it to him. "I've missed holding you, Lily. But you've had a lot of trauma in the past several days and I won't take advantage of that. I came in here to comfort you and I promise that's all that's going to happen."

"You wouldn't be taking advantage of the situation," she said, realizing that her decision had already been made. "I want you to make me forget that, outside the doors of this house, there's a world waiting to intrude." She kissed his strong jaw. "I want you to make love to me, Daniel."

* * *

To find out more about Desire's upcoming books and to chat with authors and editors, become a fan of Harlequin Desire on Facebook www.facebook.com/HarlequinDesire or follow us on Twitter www.twitter.com/desireeditors!

Dear Reader,

When I was invited to write the first book in the new Dynasties miniseries, I was absolutely thrilled. I love working with other authors on these special projects and this one was no different. I mean, who wouldn't enjoy collaborating with such talented ladies?

And as impossible as it might seem, as I wrote *Sex, Lies and the Southern Belle,* my enthusiasm grew even more. Researching Charleston, South Carolina, and specifically the historic homes in the Battery, I fell in love with the antebellum architecture and the beauty of a city so rich with history.

That's one of the reasons the antebellum mansion Lily inherits on Battery Street plays a major role in the telling of their story. As grand as any castle, the gorgeous historic home is where Lily and Daniel work to overcome the secrets of the past and together find a love that will stand the test of time.

As you read about the modern South and get acquainted with all of the Kincaid siblings, it is my fervent hope that you enjoy these stories as much as we, the authors, enjoyed writing them.

All the best,

Kathie DeNosky

KATHIE DeNOSKY

SEX, LIES AND THE SOUTHERN BELLE

Harlequin®

Desire

Special thanks and acknowledgment to Kathie DeNosky
for her contribution to the
Dynasties: The Kincaids miniseries.

ISBN-13: 978-0-373-73145-9

SEX, LIES AND THE SOUTHERN BELLE

Recycling programs
for this product may
not exist in your area.

KATHIE DeNOSKY

lives in her native southern Illinois with her big, lovable Bernese mountain dog, Nemo. Writing highly sensual stories with a generous amount of humor, Kathie's books have appeared on the Waldenbooks bestseller list and received a Write Touch Readers Award and a National Readers' Choice Award. Kathie enjoys going to rodeos, traveling to research settings for her books and listening to country music. Readers may contact Kathie at P.O. Box 2064, Herrin, Illinois 62948-5264 or email her at kathie@kathiedenosky.com. They can also visit her website, www.kathiedenosky.com.

This book is dedicated to the wonderful authors I worked with on this miniseries. It was a real pleasure, ladies!

And to Charles Griemsman. I look forward to working with you on many more in the future.

* * *

Don't miss a single book in this series!

Dynasties: The Kincaids
New money. New passions. Old secrets.

One

A knot began to form in Lily Kincaid's stomach as she looked around the conference table at her family and the three strangers who had attended her father's funeral the day before. They were gathered for the reading of Reginald Kincaid's will and as difficult as it was to believe her beloved father was gone, the fact that he had led a secret double life for the past three decades was almost impossible for her to grasp. It was just beyond comprehension to think that he'd had a second family up in Greenville all these years.

When Harold Parsons, her father's attorney, walked into the room with a thick file and sat down at the head of the table, then removed several envelopes and papers from the folder, her apprehension grew. She hated that her father had been taken from her, hated that his life's work was about to be divided up into shares. More than that, she hated that the perception she had of him had been nothing more than an illusion—an illusion that had been shattered with seemingly no way for it to ever be repaired.

"Before we begin, I would like to express my sincere condolences for your loss," Mr. Parsons said, his normally gruff voice softened with sincerity. "I knew Reginald for many years and will sorely miss his sense of humor and quick wit. I can remember the time—"

Lily bit her lower lip to keep it from trembling when the man claiming to be her half brother, Jack Sinclair, rudely cleared his throat and glanced at his watch as if he wanted to hurry things along. How could a man as warm and loving as her father had been have spawned such a cold, unfeeling son?

Her oldest brother RJ's scowl was formidable. "In a hurry to be somewhere, Sinclair?"

"As a matter of fact, I am," Jack stated flatly. "How long is this going to take, Parsons?"

Mr. Parsons's bushy white eyebrows met in a disapproving frown above his reading glasses. "It will take as long as it takes, young man."

"Please don't, Jack," Angela Sinclair begged, her voice trembling as she placed her hand on her son's arm. Her chin-length blond hair swayed slightly as she shook her head. "Please don't make this any more difficult than it already is."

If circumstances had been different, Lily would have probably felt sorry for the woman. It had been apparent yesterday at the funeral and today as they sat awaiting the reading of the will that she was taking the death of Reginald Kincaid extremely hard. But considering the nurse had been her father's mistress for the past thirty years and had shown up to mourn his death as if she and her sons were a legitimate part of the family, it was almost more than Lily could bear. Angela Sinclair either didn't realize or didn't care about what a shock and devastation it would be for the Kincaid family.

"You'll have to excuse my brother's impatience," Alan Sinclair spoke up, giving Lily and her family a sympathetic smile. "I'm afraid Jack is still trying to come to grips with Reginald's death."

Angela's youngest son, Alan, seemed to be the exact opposite of his older half-brother in every way. While Jack was tall, with dark hair, blue eyes and a cold, ruthless demeanor, Alan was shorter, had dark blond hair and hazel eyes like his mother, and appeared to be sympathetic to the shock and disbelief the Kincaids were going through. Not only were they having to cope with the death of their father, possibly by his own hand, they had been blindsided by the ugly truth of his clandestine life.

"Don't apologize for me," Jack growled, turning his hard stare on the younger man. There was such animosity in his expression, it was obvious there was no love lost between the two. "I have nothing to be sorry about."

"Enough!" RJ said, his voice deadly. Turning to the lawyer, he nodded. "Please continue, Mr. Parsons."

"If Sinclair doesn't want to stick around for the details, I'm sure you can send him a letter outlining what our father wished to leave him," Matt said, backing up RJ.

Only a few years older than herself, her brother Matt had already seen his share of heartache. It had been only a year since he had buried his wife, Grace, and been left to raise their young son, Flynn, on his own. Losing their father so soon after her passing had to bring up some very painful memories for him.

Lily glanced at her mother to see how she was holding up through this latest upheaval. The epitome of a true Southern lady, Elizabeth Kincaid had maintained an elegant calm about her throughout this whole ordeal that Lily couldn't help but envy. It appeared her mother was faring much better than Lily and her two sisters. Laurel, Lily's oldest sister, kept dabbing at her tears with a lace-edged hankie, while Kara looked as if she was in a state of total shock.

"Please continue, Harold," her mother said, smoothing a strand of short, dark auburn hair into place.

"Very well, Miss Elizabeth," Mr. Parsons said, using "miss" the way most older Southern gentlemen did with any lady, single or married. He read aloud the preliminary legalese, then clearing his throat, began to go through the list of her father's assets. "'Regarding my personal properties, I would like for them to be divided as such. To my son RJ, I leave the Great Oak Lodge in the Smoky Mountains. To my daughter Laurel, I leave my beach house on the Outer Banks. To my daughter Kara, I leave my vacation home on Hilton Head Island. To my son Matthew, I leave the Kincaid family farmhouse where we used to spend holidays. And to my daughter Lily, I leave the Colonel Samuel Beauchamp House in the Battery.'"

Tears filled Lily's eyes. Her father had known how much she loved the historic homes in the Battery. It was one of the prettiest sections in Charleston and quite possibly the entire state of South Carolina. But she had been completely unaware that he owned one of the stately mansions in that area.

After outlining the money and properties her father wished to bequeath to Elizabeth and Angela, Mr. Parsons added, "When Reginald updated his will, he wrote these letters and asked me to give them to you at this time." He passed each person in the room, except Elizabeth, a sealed envelope with their name on the front before he continued, "As for Reginald's business holdings, they are to be divided up as follows. 'RJ, Laurel, Kara, Matthew and Lily are each to receive nine percent interest in The Kincaid Group. My oldest son, Jack Sinclair, will receive forty-five percent interest.'"

Silence reigned for several long, uncomfortable moments as the gravity of her father's last wishes sank in.

"What the hell!" RJ's expression was a mixture of barely suppressed fury and total disbelief.

Lily gasped and the knot in her stomach turned to a sickening ache. How could their father do that to his children and especially to RJ, his oldest legitimate son? RJ had worked tirelessly for years as the executive vice president of The Kincaid Group and had been led to believe he would one day take over as president of the vast enterprise when their father decided it was time for him to retire. The news that their father had given the majority of the shares in the family business to Jack Sinclair was hard for all the Kincaid children to take, but it had to be completely devastating for RJ.

"That's only ninety percent," RJ said, his frown formidable. "Where's the other ten?"

Mr. Parsons shook his head. "Due to attorney/client confidentiality, I'm not at liberty to say."

The room erupted with heated allegations and threats

of legal retaliation from both sides of the table and Lily felt as if the walls were closing in on her. She knew if she didn't leave, she was going to be physically ill.

"I need…some air," she said to no one in particular.

Rising to her feet, she stuffed the unopened letter from her father into her purse and blindly ran from the room. She wasn't certain whether it was the news of her father's complete betrayal of his legitimate family or the new life growing inside her that caused her to feel sick, but she had to escape the law office.

As she hurried down the hall to the reception area, she wasn't paying attention and suddenly ran into someone standing as if rooted to the spot. Strong hands immediately came down on her shoulders to keep her from falling and when she looked up, her heart skipped several beats.

Of all the people she could have met up with in the law office, why did she have to run headlong into the owner and CEO of Addison Industries?

Daniel Addison was not only The Kincaid Group's fiercest business competitor, he was the father of her unborn child. A baby he knew absolutely nothing about.

"Where's the fire, sweetheart?" Daniel asked as he steadied the woman who, in the past couple of weeks, had treated him as if he had the plague.

"I need…air," Lily said, her voice barely more than a whisper.

Her unnatural pallor and the desperate look haunting her vibrant blue eyes caused his heart to stall. Yesterday afternoon when he attended Reginald Kincaid's funeral, he had seen her upset. But this went beyond the grief of losing a loved one. Lily looked as if her whole world was crashing down around her.

"Come on," he said, placing his arm around her shoulders and leading her toward the office exit.

"My family... I can't leave," she gasped.

Stopping at the receptionist's desk, he quickly told the woman he would call and reschedule his appointment, then instructed her to get word to the Kincaid family that he was taking Lily home. As he led her out the double glass doors and onto the sidewalk, he watched her gulp in the cool January air and knew that she was seconds away from losing her breakfast. Guiding her over to a trash can, he held her long, red hair back while she was sick.

"Please, go away and let me die in peace," she said when she finally raised her head.

"You're not going to die, Lily," he said, gently cupping her chin with one hand while he wiped the tears from her eyes with his handkerchief.

"I'm pretty sure you're wrong." She took a deep breath. "Right now I feel like death...would be a blessing."

"Did you drive your car?" he asked.

"No, I rode...with Momma," she said, her voice sounding a bit more steady.

He put his arm around her and tucked her to his side as he ushered her toward the parking garage across the street. "Good. I won't have to send someone back to get it."

"I can't leave," she said, starting to turn back toward the law offices of Parsons, Gilbert and Humbolt.

He held her firmly to his side. "This isn't negotiable, Lily. You're upset to the point of making yourself sick."

Opening the passenger door of his diamond-white Mercedes for her, Daniel nodded toward the inside of the car. "Get in. I'm taking you home."

"You're being a bully about this," she said stubbornly.

Daniel shook his head. "No, I'm making an executive decision. Now, will you please get into the car or am I going to have to pick you up and put you there?"

She glared at him. "You wouldn't."

"Try me, sweetheart."

They stared at each other for several seconds in a test of wills before she finally moved to sit down in the leather bucket seat. "Fine. Take me home and then you can be on your way."

He closed the door and walked around the car to slide into the driver's seat. "We'll see about that."

Considering her emotions at the moment, Daniel wasn't about to upset her further by telling her that he wasn't leaving her alone until he was certain she was going to be okay. He might be many things—ruthless in business, arrogant and fierce when he was in competition for a new client and jaded about most things in life—but he wasn't an uncaring bastard who left an obviously distraught female to fend for herself. Especially when that female was Lily Kincaid.

For reasons he couldn't explain, he had been drawn to her from the moment he laid eyes on her last fall at the Children's Hospital Autumn Charity Ball that his mother had helped organize. Young, vivacious and with a zest for life that he found utterly charming, he had introduced himself and asked her to dance, then asked her out to dinner. He hadn't really expected her to say yes, considering the thirteen-year difference in their ages, but to his delight she had accepted. That had been over three months ago and until the past couple of weeks, they had seen each other almost every night.

When he realized that Lily had fallen asleep, Daniel reached over to cover her delicate hand with his. He hadn't intended for things to progress between them so quickly, but he couldn't really say he was sorry they had. She was the most exciting woman he had ever met and the time they spent together had made him feel more alive and less cynical than he had in years. What he couldn't understand was why out of the clear blue sky, she stopped taking his calls and started making excuses not to go out with him.

As he turned the car into the driveway and drove around the Kincaid family home to the carriage house where Lily had an apartment, Daniel shook his head. He didn't know what had happened or why she suddenly wanted nothing to do with him, but he had every intention of finding out.

Parking the car, he reached over to trail his fingers along her smooth cheek. "You're home, sweetheart."

Her eyes fluttered open and she slowly sat up straight to look around. "Thank you for bringing me home, Daniel. I'm sure you have somewhere else you would rather be."

Before she had the chance to reach for the handle, he was out of the car and opening the door for her. "Give me your key," he said as he helped her from the vehicle.

"Really, I'll be fine." She shook her head. "You don't have to see me in."

"What kind of gentleman would I be if I didn't see you safely inside?" he asked, smiling.

For the first time since running into her in the law

office, she looked him directly in the eye. "Give me a break, Mr. Addison. It's midmorning and I seriously doubt that there's a safety issue for you to be concerned with."

He reached up to trail his index finger along her creamy cheek. "So now it's Mr. Addison? I thought we were a lot closer than that, sweetheart."

"I...uh, at one time...I suppose we were," she said, clearly uncomfortable with his observation.

Daniel had heard about someone looking as if they were a deer caught in headlights, but until that moment he hadn't seen it for himself. But that was the only way to describe the expression on Lily's pretty face. She looked trapped and desperate.

The question was, why? What had made her so clearly uncomfortable about being in his presence?

Unfortunately, he was going to have to bide his time until she was feeling a little more in control before he got to the bottom of what was going on with her and why she had ended their affair. The past few days had been a nightmare for her and her family and he wasn't going to add more stress by interrogating her as to what had changed between them.

Placing his hand at the small of her back, he felt a slight tremor course through her and instinctively knew it had nothing to do with the mild winter weather Charleston was experiencing. Good. At least she hadn't developed a complete immunity to him.

"I know that all this has been extremely hard on you, Lily," he said, meaning it. "For my own peace of mind, I want to see that you're all right before I leave."

"There's nothing I can say that's going to dissuade you, is there?" she asked, sighing heavily.

KATHIE DeNOSKY   17

"No."

She looked more tired and world-weary than he had ever seen her and he hated that the events of the past several days had suppressed her fun-loving, free spirit. Whether she realized it or not, Lily needed someone to help her get through one of the toughest times in her life and he had every intention of being the one she turned to.

"Why don't you sit down and put your feet up while I make coffee?" he said when they walked into the living room and he helped her out of her coat.

"No caffeine for me." Her long wavy hair swayed as she shook her head. "I, um, haven't been sleeping well."

"I can understand that." He nodded as he removed his overcoat, then guided her to the couch. "You've been through a lot in the past few days, sweetheart."

"You have no idea," she said as she sank onto the cushions. Tears filled her pretty blue eyes as she looked up at him. "Why did he do it?"

If the account of Reginald's death in the newspaper had been correct, the man had used one of the antique guns in his collection to take his own life. Daniel knew for a fact that Lily and her father had been very close and his apparent suicide had to have been extremely difficult for her to cope with.

"I can't tell you why things happened the way they did, Lily," he said, sitting down beside her to take her into his arms. "It might never be clear why your dad felt compelled to end things in such a drastic way. But once the shock has worn off, I'm sure you'll be able to put this behind you and look back at the good times you shared together."

She stubbornly shook her head. "I'm not so sure. Not

when everything I thought I knew about my father has turned out to be a total lie."

He had meant to console her, not upset her further. "Give yourself some time. Right now your emotions are still too raw to see things clearly."

"You don't understand, Daniel." She pulled away from him to meet his gaze head-on. "I mean literally—everything about Daddy was a lie."

Something about her impassioned statement told him there was a lot more to the story than what the media had reported and she needed to get it out or risk going into emotional meltdown. "What leads you to believe that, Lily?"

She hesitated for a moment as first one tear, then another, spilled down her cheeks. "I might as well tell you. It's going to be the talk of Charleston by the end of the week."

"I'm listening."

"Did you notice that older blonde woman and the two men with her that sat just behind my family at the funeral?" she asked.

He nodded. "Are they relatives from out of town?"

"No. Yes." She swiped at her tears with the back of her hand. "To tell you the truth, I'm not sure what I should call them."

"Slow down, Lily." He didn't like that she was becoming more agitated. "Who are they?"

"That was my father's second family," she said as if the words tasted bitter. "For the past thirty years, all of his out-of-town business trips were nothing more than excuses to travel up to Greenville to spend time with that woman and her two sons."

Of all the things Lily could have told him about

Reginald Kincaid, that was the last thing Daniel expected. "Let me get this straight," he said slowly, trying to digest the revelation. "Your father had another wife and two kids up in Greenville that you're just finding out about?"

Lily nodded. "Actually, Angela Sinclair was my father's first love and her oldest son, Jack, is my half brother. Her youngest son, Alan, belonged to her late husband."

"Jack Sinclair is your half brother?" He had heard of the man and the resounding success Sinclair had made of his start-up company, Carolina Shipping, but Daniel hadn't had the opportunity to meet the man or do business with him. "But didn't you just say he was the oldest? How could his younger brother belong to another man?"

"My dad and Angela were involved when they were very young, but my grandparents didn't think she was the right type of girl for him," Lily explained, rising to pace the floor. "The way I understand it, my grandfather was building his shipping business into what The Kincaid Group is today. He and my grandmother wanted my father to marry someone who could further their standing with the social set of Charleston."

Daniel knew all too well how the bastions of Southern high society worked. His mother came from old money and was well-entrenched in the ranks of the social elite. She and her so-called friends looked down on anyone whose fortune didn't go back at least four generations, or whose family tree didn't include at least one or two officers from the Civil War.

"As an act of rebellion, Daddy joined the army to escape their matchmaking and since he was in a Special

Ops unit, there were months at a time that no one could communicate with him," Lily went on. "From what was said yesterday at the funeral, Angela tried to get word to him that she was expecting his child, but by the time Daddy was wounded and sent back here, Angela had seemingly dropped off the face of the earth. He thought she got tired of waiting for him and moved on."

"So when he couldn't find her, he gave in to his parents and married your mother?" Daniel guessed.

Lily nodded. "The Winthrops were an old, well-established family in Charleston, but by the mid-seventies their fortune had dwindled to almost nothing and they were desperate to maintain their lifestyle and place within their social circle."

Although Daniel hated the snobbery and pretentiousness of it all, it was the social order he had been born into and knew exactly how it worked. He had seen many of the old Southern families swallow their pride and encourage their sons or daughters to marry one of the nouveau riche. If they didn't, their lack of means effectively ostracized them from the wealthy social community.

"So it was advantageous for both families when your mother and father got married," he said, nodding. "Your dad's parents went up several notches on the social register and your mother's family gained someone to help them financially, as well as prop up their position in high society."

"I think that sums it up perfectly," Lily agreed.

"How did your dad and Angela get back together?" Daniel asked, wondering how Reginald had managed to find the woman after all those years when he hadn't been able to before. "And what about her husband? Where does he figure into the equation?"

"Apparently, her parents gave her a choice of marrying Richard Sinclair or giving up her child." Lily shook her head. "Given no other choice, I would have done the same thing and married a man I didn't love to keep my baby."

Daniel frowned. "What about Sinclair? What happened to him?"

"After they married and moved out of state, Angela gave birth to Jack and then several years later, she and Richard Sinclair had a son they named Alan." She shrugged one slender shoulder. "I'm not sure if it was an accident or if he became ill, but Richard died not long after that."

"So he's out of the picture and your dad finds Angela again," Daniel thought aloud.

Lily sighed heavily. "I don't know how he did it, but when he found her and discovered that she had given birth to his son, Daddy set up her and the two boys in a house in Greenville. Apparently she had been struggling to make ends meet on her nurse's salary and life got a lot easier for them when Daddy came on the scene. After that, he starting going on frequent business trips, which were actually visits to spend time with her and her sons."

Daniel shook his head as he tried to digest the story. "And you found this out yesterday at the funeral?"

A tear slid down her cheek and she bit her lower lip to keep it from trembling a moment before she answered. "Y-yes. But what we learned this morning at the reading of the will just compounded the hurt and betrayal we were feeling about his second family."

"What's that, sweetheart?" He couldn't imagine how the situation could get more complicated.

"Daddy left the majority of The Kincaid Group to Jack Sinclair, while my siblings and I were each given nine percent interest," she said swiping another tear from her cheek. "My father led RJ and Matthew to believe they would be running TKG one day. How could he betray Momma this way? And, for that matter, how could he betray all of us?"

Daniel didn't hesitate to stand up, walk over to her and take Lily into his arms. He knew how crushing the loss of her father had to have been for her, but finding out that he had led a secret life for so many years, then handed control of his business to someone the family hadn't even been aware existed had to increase the emotional pain ten times over. Pulling her against him, he held her as he tried to lend her his strength and support.

His compassion seemed to open the floodgates and he tightened his embrace as she sobbed against his chest. He didn't like seeing a woman cry. It always made him uncomfortable and at a loss as to what he should do. Lily's tears made him feel more useless than ever. He wanted to help, wanted to make the hurt she was suffering go away.

Unfortunately, only the passage of time could heal the pain and anguish of losing a loved one. He knew that firsthand from losing his own father to a heart attack fifteen years ago. But the disillusionment she was feeling over her father's indisputable betrayal might never go away.

"I'm okay now," she finally said, pulling from his arms.

"Are you sure?" he asked, reluctant to let her go. Although he hated what she was going through, he liked having Lily in his arms.

Nodding, she walked over to the couch, then curled up in the corner of it. "Thank you for bringing me home, Daniel. But I'm really tired. Could you please lock the door as you let yourself out?"

He had been dismissed and it didn't sit any better this time than it had for the past couple of weeks. But he knew she was completely exhausted from lack of sleep and the emotional turmoil she had been going through. Now wasn't the time to get into why she suddenly had no time for him.

"I'll be back this evening to check on you," he said, reaching for his overcoat.

"I appreciate your concern, but I'll be okay," she said, hiding a yawn behind her delicate hand. She snuggled down to lay her head on a plush pillow. "There's no need for you to go to the trouble of stopping by later. Really, I'll be fine."

Shrugging into his coat, he shook his head as he started toward the door. "It's not a problem. I'll pick something up for dinner and see you around six."

He expected her to protest, but when he turned around, Daniel discovered that Lily's eyes were closed and she was sound asleep. Good, he thought as he walked over to the couch to remove a colorful crocheted afghan from the back, then covered her with it. At least she couldn't tell him not to bother.

"Get some rest, sweetheart," he said quietly as he leaned down to kiss her forehead. "I'll be back in a few hours."

She murmured what sounded like his name, but she

didn't wake up to protest his returning and, as far as he was concerned, that was as good as her consent.

As he let himself out the front door and walked to his car, Daniel knew he was taking advantage of the situation. Lily had made it perfectly clear that she wanted nothing more to do with him and up until this morning, he had respected her wishes and backed off. But for some reason, he couldn't let it go, couldn't walk away without an explanation of why she'd had a change of heart about their affair.

Opening the driver's door and sliding in behind the steering wheel, he sat and stared at the carriage house for several long minutes. Considering his feelings on love and relationships, he was mystified why it even mattered. Maybe it was the fact that Lily had broken things off between them without telling him why and he was allowing curiosity to get the better of him. Or more likely, it was his stubborn pride that wouldn't allow him to drop the matter without making her tell him what had caused her to stop seeing him.

Whatever the reason, he was going to help Lily weather the emotional storm of losing her father and the family scandal that was about to erupt. Then he fully intended to get his answers from her and move on.

TWO

After waking up to find Daniel had done as she asked and left her alone, Lily frowned at her feelings of disappointment. "Get a grip on yourself," she muttered as she pushed the afghan aside and sat up.

Daniel Addison was all wrong for her and the sooner she came to terms with that fact, the better off she would be. She had known when they first started seeing each other that it would end one day. It had to. They were exact opposites and wanted entirely different things out of life.

She wanted love, marriage and babies. But after going through a bitter divorce from his wife, Charisma, several years ago, those were the last things Daniel wanted. All he cared about were short-term affairs devoid of deep emotions, commitment and children. And if Lily hadn't known that from the gossip she had heard at some of the social functions around Charleston, she had certainly found out when his mother took great pleasure in telling her.

A shiver slithered down Lily's spine when she thought of how poorly she had been treated at the dinner party she and Daniel attended at Addison House, just before Christmas. His mother was, without a shadow of a doubt, the coldest, most unpleasant woman Lily had ever had the misfortune to meet. The woman had even gone so far as to accuse Lily of trying to elevate her social standing by being associated with Daniel—implying that because her father's fortune didn't go back several generations, Lily wasn't worthy of circulating among those considered to come from "old money."

She shuddered at the thought of ever being near the woman again. But more upsetting was that Charlotte Addison was the paternal grandmother of Lily's child.

Lily nibbled on her lower lip as she tried to calm the butterflies in her stomach. She was having Daniel's baby and at some point she was going to have to tell him. But how? How was she going to break the news to a man who had no interest in ever having a child of his own that whether he wanted to or not, he was going to be a daddy? And considering his feelings about children, would he try to get her to end the pregnancy?

She placed a protective hand over her still flat stomach. She truly didn't think he would ask that of her, but it wouldn't matter if he did. This baby was hers and she loved it with all of her heart.

Rising to her feet, she wandered into her studio and glanced at the drawings for the latest children's book she was illustrating. Children were so very important to her and she couldn't imagine anyone not wanting to have a child to enrich their life.

She released a shuddering breath. It would just be his loss, she thought sadly. Whether he wanted anything to do with the baby or not, it was only right to let him know about her pregnancy, and as soon as she found a good time, she fully intended to do just that.

As she stood there pondering how to go about telling him that he had fathered a child, the phone rang. When she answered, she wasn't at all surprised to hear her oldest sister's concerned voice.

"Are you all right, Lily?" Laurel asked.

"I'm fine now," Lily said, smiling.

She loved her family and the closeness they shared. But she hadn't told them about her pregnancy and she wasn't sure how to broach the subject. It was a given they would be supportive, but they were all busy with their own lives and she hated to add her problems to theirs. As public relations director for The Kincaid Group, Laurel was going to have to handle the media frenzy the scandal was sure to cause, as well as get ready for her upcoming wedding. Thankfully, their sister Kara was using her skills as a wedding and party planner to pull it all together for Laurel, but at the same time she was booked up with jobs for her thriving business, Prestige Events.

Lily could always turn to her brothers for advice, but they were no less busy than her sisters. Until today, RJ had his hands full being interim CEO of The Kincaid Group since their father's death, but she suspected he would soon be turning his attention to a legal battle as he tried to regain control of the business now that Jack

Sinclair held the majority of the shares. That left Matt. Poor Matt was so busy trying to juggle his job as director of New Business at TKG and being a single father, that he didn't have time for himself, let alone to give her advice on how she should handle this new twist in her life.

"You left so quickly this morning, I wanted to make sure that you're feeling better," Laurel went on.

"I just needed some air," Lily said, sorry for the worry she had caused her sibling. "I still can't believe that Daddy left the biggest part of the company to that awful man."

"I know," Laurel agreed, sounding as disillusioned as Lily. "We're looking into finding who owns the missing ten percent. If we can get whoever it is to vote with us, then as a whole, we'll have controlling interest in TKG. And at this point, that's imperative. After you left, Jack smugly told RJ and Matt that he expected a full report of assets, expenses, projected growth and a comprehensive customer list for TKG by the end of the month."

"What is he going to do with it?" Lily asked, alarmed. Did he intend to sell his shares back to the Kincaids at a ridiculously high price? Or was he planning to split the company and sell it off piece by piece?

"At this point, it's anyone's guess what he'll do with the information." Laurel's sigh echoed in Lily's ear. "But RJ and Matt are going to be busy working practically around the clock to get things together."

"I can only imagine how frustrated and angry RJ feels about all this." RJ was not the type of man to put up with Jack Sinclair's arrogance any longer than it took him to find a way to defeat him.

"RJ doesn't have a choice," Laurel said. "But I don't want you to worry about any of this, Lily. RJ and Matt will figure it out and if there's a way for us to regain control of TKG, they'll find it."

"Asking me not to worry is like asking me to make the sun rise in the west tomorrow morning. But I do promise I'll try." A knock on the front door had her walking out of her studio. "I have to go, Laurel. Someone's at the door. I'll talk to you tomorrow. Love you."

"Love you, too," Laurel said, ending the conversation.

Lily put the cordless unit on the charger, then continued to the door. It was probably one of her other siblings dropping by to check on her. After the way she'd fled Mr. Parsons's office this morning, she really wasn't surprised. Since she was the youngest in the family, her brothers and sisters had always watched out for her and she loved them all the more for it.

But when she opened the door, she found Daniel standing on the other side with a large paper bag in one hand and a bottle of wine in the other. "I was beginning to think you might still be napping," he said as he brushed past her and walked toward the dining area at the opposite end of the room.

"What are you doing here, Daniel?" she asked, closing the door to follow him.

Looking over his shoulder, he gave her an indulgent smile. "Don't you remember? I told you I would be back with dinner around six."

She frowned. "I remember telling you that you didn't need to bother stopping by, but I don't recall anything about you bringing dinner."

"You might have fallen asleep by that time," he said,

pulling cartons of delicious-smelling food from the paper bag to place them on the table.

"Might have?" She shook her head. "It's more likely that you purposely waited until I had gone to sleep to mention bringing dinner."

He shrugged as he removed his coat, then walked over to lay it on the back of one of the armchairs. "Either way, I did mention it." He returned to the table and picked up the bottle of wine. "Besides, you have to eat and I didn't think you would feel like making something for yourself."

Even though the food he had brought smelled heavenly and she was ravenous, she wasn't willing to give in so easily. "I might have plans," she said stubbornly.

"But you don't." He gave her a smile that caused her to feel warm all over. "Now, why don't we sit down and enjoy this before it gets cold?"

If there was one thing about Daniel Addison that she had learned in the past several months, it was that he never lacked confidence. She only wished she could say the same for herself, especially now that she was going to have to find a way to tell him about her pregnancy.

When he reached for two wineglasses on top of her small liquor cabinet, she shook her head. "I'm going to have a glass of milk."

He nodded as he removed the corkscrew from the cabinet drawer and popped the cork on the wine bottle. "Considering how sick you were this morning, that's probably a good idea."

She didn't comment as she walked into the kitchen and opened the refrigerator. It would probably be best if he was sitting down when she told him the reason behind her illness this morning and why she wasn't drinking wine with her meal.

When she returned to the dining area, she wasn't surprised that he had gotten plates from the china cabinet and was setting their places at the table. He was a man who took charge and was hands on when he saw something that had to be done. A tiny tingle coursed through her when she remembered his hands on her and the magic he created whenever he...

"Lily, are you all right?" he asked, bringing her back to the present.

"Um...of course, why do you ask?" She had to stop thinking about what they had shared in the past because there was absolutely no future in it.

A shadow of concern clouded his dark blue eyes. "You're not acting like yourself, sweetheart. You seem distracted by something."

The endearment Daniel always used made her long to go back a few months to when they first began seeing each other and everything was much simpler. His mother hadn't said those mean things to her and she hadn't known that her beloved father had been leading a double life since before she was born.

"I was just thinking about how everything was before Christmas." She shook her head as the gravity of all that had happened settled across her shoulders. "We had no way of knowing that it would be our last holiday with Daddy or that we would start out the new year with his funeral and a family scandal that will undoubtedly be talked about for years to come."

When Daniel took her glass of milk from her to set it on the table, then reached out to wrap his arms around her, Lily placed her hands on his broad chest to push away from him. Her whole world had changed in ways she could have never imagined and it was almost more than she could take in. But she couldn't allow herself to be drawn back under his spell.

"Please, Daniel," she said, trying to hold herself away from him.

"Hush, sweetheart," he whispered. "You need someone to lean on right now."

"Not literally," she said, unwilling to give up so easily.

His deep chuckle sent a shiver straight through her. "I think literal has its merits."

Unfortunately, Daniel was much stronger and the more she pushed, the closer he drew her to him. Suddenly too emotionally exhausted to resist any longer, she rested her head against his broad chest. Just for a moment, she wanted to forget that the past few weeks had happened and pretend that her life was the same as it had always been—carefree and happy.

But the feel of his hard muscles against her cheek, the steady beat of his heart and the solid strength of his arms around her, caused a longing to build inside her that had nothing to do with comfort and support. She had missed this man more than she had thought was possible, and it would be in her best interest to put distance between them.

Looking up into his navy eyes, Lily started to pull away, but just as a night creature often became trapped in the headlights of an oncoming car, she couldn't seem to look away as he slowly began to lower his head. He was going to kiss her and, for the life of her, she couldn't remember why she shouldn't let him. But the sudden rumbling of her stomach reminded both of them that she hadn't eaten anything since breakfast.

Daniel took a deep breath, kissed her forehead and smiled. "It would probably be a good idea if you eat something, sweetheart."

"I think you're right," she said, thankful that hunger had intervened and kept her from doing something she would regret later. The last thing she needed to do was fall under his spell again. Stepping back, she turned to pull out one of the chairs at the table and sat down. "What smells so delicious?"

"When I stopped by Miss Pauline's Southern Cupboard, I wasn't sure which you would prefer, baked chicken or roast beef," he said, seating himself at the head of the table. "So I got both."

"I'm positively starved," she said, meaning it. She might have been sick every morning for the past couple of weeks, but every evening, her appetite seemed to return with a vengeance. "I think I'll have a little of both. I love Miss Pauline's food."

"We also have mashed potatoes with gravy, green beans, corn fritters and fresh-made corn bread," he said, reaching for her plate. "And be sure to save room for apple pie."

"It all sounds heavenly," she said, watching him fill her plate. "I have some vanilla ice cream in the freezer that would be fantastic with the pie."

They both fell silent for several minutes as they enjoyed the delicious food. But the longer Daniel watched Lily eat, the more fascinated he became. They'd shared many meals, but he didn't think he had ever seen her quite so hungry. She was eating like a longshoreman after a full day's work at the docks of Port Charleston.

"When was the last time you ate?" he asked, watching her put another corn fritter on her plate, then reach for the carton of green beans.

She nibbled on her lower lip a moment as if trying to decide what to say. "I couldn't stand the thought of breakfast this morning," she said tentatively. "I only had a few crackers and a cup of tea. Then I slept through lunch and only woke up about an hour before you arrived with dinner."

He could understand her inability to eat earlier in the day. Knowing that she was going to come face-to-face with her father's second family for the reading of his will was enough to cause anyone to lose their appetite. And as exhausted as she had been, Daniel wasn't at all surprised that she had missed lunch. But it appeared she was making up for it now.

"Don't forget to leave room for the pie and ice cream," he said, smiling as he watched her enjoy another bite of roast beef.

"I know that the amount of butter Miss Pauline uses when she cooks is probably not the most healthy. But she has the best food in South Carolina." He watched Lily smile blissfully as a forkful of the buttery mashed potatoes disappeared into her mouth.

"I don't think it does any harm to eat like this occasionally," he said, amazed that she still had room for another bite of corn bread. "It's having food like this every day that isn't good for you. It clogs arteries and can add several pounds."

As soon as he said it, Daniel wished he could call the words back. If he had learned nothing else in his disastrous marriage, it was definitely not to mention gaining weight to a woman.

Lily slowly laid her fork on the edge of her plate

and gave him a penetrating look. "Do I look as if I've gained weight?"

Damn, Addison! Way to stick your foot in your mouth. How are you going to talk your way out of this one? Mentioning weight gain to a woman was the best way in the world to have her hand a man his head on a silver platter.

"I didn't say you looked like you had gained weight," he said, choosing his words carefully. "Just that if a person ate this way all the time, they would."

Instead of tearing into him for mentioning weight at all, as he thought she would, to his surprise Lily smiled as she shrugged one shoulder. "I suppose gaining a little weight isn't the end of the world."

It was all Daniel could do to keep his mouth from dropping open. If he had made the same blunder with Charisma, his ex-wife would have made his life a living hell for at least a month and it would have cost him an expensive piece of jewelry or a whole new wardrobe of designer clothes to pay for his sins. Then, every time they had any kind of disagreement, she would have dragged his comment on gaining weight into the fray. But Lily seemed to take it in stride and didn't act at all concerned about it. Amazing!

Deciding there was no sense in pushing his luck any further, he stood up to carry their plates into the kitchen. "I'll get the pie and ice cream."

"I'll help," she said, starting to rise from her chair.

Smiling, he shook his head. "Just sit there and relax. You've had a rough day and although I'm lost about most things in a kitchen, I'm pretty sure I can handle dipping a scoop of ice cream onto a piece of pie."

When he returned a couple of minutes later and

placed the dessert in front of her, Lily smiled as she picked up her spoon. "For a man who doesn't know his way around a kitchen, you did pretty well. It looks delicious."

He chuckled. "I'm afraid this is as far as my culinary skills go. Why do you think I took you out to eat all those times?"

"I really hadn't thought much about it," she said, closing her eyes as she savored the combined flavors of vanilla, cinnamon and apple.

As Daniel watched, her expression changed to one of pure pleasure and he couldn't help but remember the times he had seen a similar look come over her as he made love to her. A spark ignited in his lower belly at the thought of how responsive she had been, how passionate.

He swallowed hard and tried to think of something innocuous. He might have succeeded had it not been for Lily slowly licking a drop of melted ice cream from her lips. The action reminded him of other talents she had with that perfect little tongue and had him shifting to relieve the mounting pressure of his suddenly too-tight trousers.

When had the simple act of eating a piece of pie become so damn erotic?

"Don't you want yours?" she asked, unaware of his wayward thoughts.

Daniel stared down at the dessert in front of him. Oh, he wanted, all right, but it wasn't pie that he was craving. It was the memory of her delicious body pressed to his that fueled his hunger and caused his mouth to feel as if it had been stuffed with cotton.

Taking a gulp of his wine, he forced his body to

relax. He had no doubt that at any other time, he would find Miss Pauline's pie quite tasty. At the moment, it might as well have been a piece of rubber on his plate.

"Are you okay?" Lily asked, reaching over to steal a spoonful of his ice cream.

Nodding, he did his best to focus on Lily and her seemingly insatiable appetite. She had finished her pie and ice cream and now it appeared she was starting on his.

"I'm not all that hungry, why don't we share?" he said, picking up his spoon. He dipped it into the melting ice cream, then held it to her lips.

Her eyes met his as she opened her mouth and he immediately knew he had made a huge error in judgment. In all of his thirty-eight years, he didn't think he had experienced anything more provocative than having her gaze locked with his as her lips slowly closed around the bite of ice cream. His libido kicked into overdrive, reminding him that it had been the better part of three weeks since they had made love.

"I really hate to cut the evening short," he said suddenly, making a show of glancing at his watch. "But I just remembered I have to make an overseas call as soon as the Japanese markets open."

Lily had been on an emotional roller coaster for the past several days, and taking advantage of a woman's vulnerability to seduce her had never been his style. But if he didn't get out of there and damn quick, that was exactly what was going to happen.

"Thank you for bringing supper," she said, placing her napkin on the table beside her plate. "It really was delicious."

"It looked as if you might have been happy with my choices," he said dryly.

Confident that he had his body back under control, Daniel rose to his feet, quickly helped Lily clear the table, then walked into the living room to find his coat. "I'll come by tomorrow to see how you're doing."

Lily followed him to the door. "Thank you for your concern, Daniel. I do appreciate it. But it really isn't necessary. It may take some time, but I'm going to be fine. Really."

It appeared she was back to giving him the brush-off and that didn't sit well with him one bit. Turning back, he didn't think twice about reaching up to run the back of his hand along her smooth cheek. As he searched her upturned face for what she might be thinking, Lily swayed ever so slightly and leaned into his touch. He could tell it wasn't a conscious action on her part, but it was all the indication he needed that she still desired him. Taking her into his arms, he gathered her to him.

"Daniel, don't—"

"Hush, sweetheart," he said, brushing her mouth with his. He intended to remind her of how responsive she had always been to his touch.

Teasing her with feathery kisses, he nibbled at her perfect lips to test her willingness to allow him to continue. When she moaned softly and brought her hands up to his chest to grasp the fabric of his shirt as if to steady herself, elated satisfaction coursed through him. Whatever her reason had been for trying to distance herself from him the past few weeks, it wasn't because she no longer wanted him.

As difficult as it was, Daniel fought the urge to deepen the kiss. He had proven his point and although he fully intended for them to become lovers once again, he wanted to build her frustration to the degree that she could no longer deny her need for him.

"I'll see you tomorrow, Lily," he said, untangling her fingers from his shirt to take a step back.

The confusion on her pretty face and the disappointment she couldn't quite hide caused him to smile and, before she had the chance to find her voice and protest, he opened the door and stepped out into the cool January night. His body throbbed with longing and Daniel knew as surely as he knew his own name, he was in for a miserable, sleepless night. But in the long run, it was going to be well worth whatever hell he had to go through to have Lily back in his life and in his bed.

He just hoped he didn't go completely insane before that happened.

Staring at the closed door, Lily couldn't believe the myriad of emotions roiling inside her. She had wanted Daniel to actually kiss her, not just tease her to the point of utter frustration. But that was exactly what had happened and her disappointment that he hadn't kissed her senseless led to a deep annoyance with herself for wishing that he had.

She shook her head as she turned to walk into the kitchen to load the dishwasher. She couldn't believe how easy it would have been for her to throw common sense out the window and lose herself in Daniel's arms. Thank heavens he had backed off and hadn't taken things any further. She wouldn't have been able to resist him and that was something she had to do at all costs. Calling a halt to their seeing each other had been one of the hardest things she had ever done, but it was the only way to ensure she didn't suffer more hurt when he found out about the baby and walked away. They wanted different things in life, and it was best to stop now before she lost her heart completely.

But that didn't explain why she had failed to let him know about the baby when he noticed her voracious appetite. It had been the perfect opportunity to explain why she ate more than usual and that she fully expected to gain weight as her pregnancy progressed.

Her pregnancy hormones had to be responsible for her mixed emotions as well as her reluctance to let him know he was going to be a father. Either that or it was the dread of telling him and knowing for certain that his interest in her would come to a swift and permanent end.

Sighing, Lily started the dishwasher and wandered into the living room. She supposed she should work on the new children's book she had been commissioned to illustrate. But when the family had been informed that her father had died of an apparent self-inflicted gunshot wound at his TKG office, she had put work on hold and hadn't been able to concentrate on it since.

She still couldn't believe all that had happened over the past several days—especially what had taken place during the reading of her father's will just that morning. But as she thought about her father's betrayal of his legitimate family, she remembered the letters Mr. Parsons had given to them. She had forgotten about them after running into Daniel at the law office.

Lily stared at her purse, which was lying on the end table, and her hand shook when she finally worked up the courage to reach for it. She wasn't at all certain she was prepared to read her father's last thoughts to her.

But then, she didn't think she would ever be ready for what was probably his final goodbye.

For several long moments after retrieving the envelope from her bag, she simply sat there holding it while she stared at her name in her father's handwriting on the front. Given all that she had learned about him in the past several days, could she even believe what he had to say to her?

Finally, she decided that whether she believed what he had written or not, the only way to know would be to open the envelope. Taking a deep breath, she turned it over and, using her fingernail, lifted the sealed flap. When she pulled out the letter and unfolded it, her breath caught on a sob when she noticed the date. It was only a few days before he died.

My dearest Lily,
One of the greatest joys in my life has always been that you thought of me as your knight in shining armor. Whether it was chasing away the monsters from your closet when you were three, kissing a skinned elbow to make the hurt go away when you were eight or listening to your hopes and dreams as you got ready to go off to college, every second of the time we spent together has been very special and I never wanted you to see me as anything but your hero. Unfortunately, Lily-girl, I'm just a man with a man's faults.

By now you've discovered that your dear old dad had feet of clay and wasn't quite the champion you thought me to be. I never meant to disappoint you and I hope one day you can find it in your heart to forgive me for my weaknesses. No matter what you hear about me and my transgressions, please know that the bond between us was not only real, but very precious to me.

One of the many things that you and I shared together was a love of the historic district of Charleston. That's why I'm leaving you the Colonel Samuel Beauchamp House in the Battery. It's one of the city's finest examples of Southern architecture and I know from the Saturday afternoons we spent in White Point Gardens when you were a child that it's your favorite. You may meet with a bit of resistance from the former owner, Charlotte Addison, but stand your ground, Lily. You're a strong, capable young woman and whatever decision you make concerning the property, I know it will be the right one for you.

I love you, Lily, and I have no doubt that without me you'll find the strength to weather whatever challenges life brings your way. From the moment you were born, you have been my little princess—the ray of sunshine that brightened my life and I feel very blessed that you are my daughter.

With love,
Daddy

Tears streamed down Lily's face as she slowly folded the letter and returned it to the envelope. Deep down she had known that the closeness between her and her father couldn't have been a lie, but the hurt and disillusionment of the past few days had overshadowed their relationship and caused her to question what she knew in her heart to be true. No matter what he had done, her father had loved her.

Unfortunately, it was going to take her some time to get past his handing over controlling interest in TKG to Jack Sinclair, while more or less cutting his legitimate children out of the picture. Lily sighed heavily. Then there was his betrayal of her mother, even though Elizabeth Kincaid didn't seem to be nearly as upset about the disturbing revelations as Lily would have thought.

"What were you thinking, Daddy?" she murmured aloud.

As she sat there wondering what her father could have possibly thought to accomplish by what she could only describe as inexcusable choices, something she had read in the letter caused her to catch her breath.

Quickly removing the letter from the envelope, she reread what her father had left her and the name of the Beauchamp mansion's former owner—Daniel's unpleasant, ill-tempered mother. Dear heavens, what had he gotten her into?

Three

After a miserable couple of hours waiting for her morning sickness to subside, Lily sat with her elbow propped on her art table, her chin cupped in her palm. She wasn't accomplishing anything by staring off into space, but she couldn't seem to settle down to work. All she had been able to think about since reading her father's letter the night before was what she was going to do with the Beauchamp property.

She had never been inside the structure, but from the outside the beautiful four-story antebellum mansion had always captured her eye. With three levels of piazzas overlooking White Point Gardens and Charleston Harbor beyond, she was almost certain that the Sullivan's Island Lighthouse and Fort Sumter could be seen in the distance.

She smiled wistfully. As a child, whenever she had

passed by the stately double house, she had imagined how wonderful it would be to stand in the cupola on top of the tall roof and pretend to be a princess, surveying her kingdom below. And now the home she had thought to be as grand as any castle was actually hers.

What on earth was she going to do with it? It was such a big house and she didn't need all that space. Of course, when the baby came there would be the two of them, but it was still going to be much more room than they would need.

As she pondered what to do with the mansion, she was reminded of her father's warning. What had he meant when he told her that she would meet with opposition from Charlotte Addison? What was that all about?

Deciding she wasn't getting anything done anyway, Lily left her art table and walked over to the laptop on her desk. With everything being accessible online these days, she should be able to find out some of the mansion's history and the connection that Daniel's mother had with the place. A few of the homes in the Battery had been passed from one generation to the next, never being occupied by anyone outside of the family who built them. A sense of dread began to settle in the pit of Lily's stomach.

Her suspicions were confirmed when the first link she clicked on was a twenty-year-old article on homes in the Battery. According to the reporter from the *Post and Courier,* Charleston's newspaper, the mansion had been in Colonel Samuel Beauchamp's family since it was built in the late 1700s. It went on to read that the home had been passed down to his descendants and, at the time the article was written, belonged to Mrs. Charlotte Beauchamp-Addison, who anticipated keeping it in the family when she eventually passed it on to her son, Daniel.

A chill traveled the length of Lily's spine. No wonder Charlotte Addison had treated her so poorly when she had shown up with Daniel at the dinner party. She obviously resented the fact that Reginald Kincaid, one of the nouveau riche, as the woman had called him, had purchased her ancestral home. Lily had been condemned simply because she was his daughter. If the mansion had meant so much to her, what could have possibly caused Charlotte to sell it to him?

Lily suddenly caught her breath. Did Daniel know about all this? Was he aware that her father had bought the home he was supposed to own one day and could that be the reason he had become interested in her to begin with? Had he hoped to somehow use his association with her to get the Beauchamp mansion back into his family?

Frowning, she nibbled on her lower lip. She didn't think that was the case. He had told her on more than one occasion that he loved the new condo he'd bought after his divorce. It was close to the Addison Industries office building and within walking distance of Charleston's French Quarter.

Trying to unravel her tangled thoughts, Lily jumped when the phone rang. "Hello Matt," she said, recognizing her brother's office number on the caller ID.

"Lily, could you do me a favor and watch Flynn one night a week for the next several weeks?" Her brother sounded rushed and she could only imagine the tremendous amount of stress he was under after hearing that

Jack Sinclair was going to be in control of The Kincaid Group.

"Of course," she said, smiling. "You know how much I love my nephew."

"Great. RJ and I are going to be working late for who knows how long and I'm trying to line up babysitters," Matt explained.

"What nights do you need me?" Lily asked. She loved spending time with Flynn and found that playing with him had inspired some of her best illustrations.

"Are you free Thursday evenings?" he asked. "Laurel is watching him Mondays and Kara has Tuesdays and Wednesdays covered."

"That's fine. What about the weekends?"

"He's going to spend Friday nights and all day on Saturdays with Mom." Lily heard him shuffle papers and realized Matt was trying to work and arrange child care at the same time. "I've already told RJ that Jack Sinclair can wait on the reports he wants until hell freezes over if need be, but Sundays are mine with Flynn and I'm not going to give that up for Sinclair or anyone else."

"Good for you," Lily said, meaning it. "Is there anything else I can do to help?"

She heard her brother sigh heavily. "Not unless you can figure out a way to add several more hours to the day."

"Sorry, Matt, but I don't think anyone has figured out how to do that just yet. What time do you need me on Thursday evenings?" When he named a time, she added, "Please take care of yourself. Whatever is going to happen, it's not worth sacrificing your health."

"Thanks, sis," he said, sounding tired. "I'll try to keep that in mind."

After ending the call, Lily started to return to her worktable to try to get something done, when the phone rang again.

"Good afternoon, sweetheart," Daniel said cheerfully. "I'm about five minutes away. Would you like to start setting the table for lunch?"

"Daniel, I'm not sure—"

"Have you eaten yet?"

"No, but—"

"Then set the table," he said, breaking the connection.

Lily stared at the phone in her hand for several seconds before placing it on the desk to go set the table. She thought about calling Daniel back and insisting that he respect her wishes to be left alone. But she did need to talk to him and try to find out how much he knew about the sale of the Beauchamp mansion to her father as well as try to find a way to tell him about the baby.

Maybe then she would know more about what kind of battle her father had gotten her into with the Addisons. And how Daniel was going to react when he learned about the baby.

As Daniel steered his Mercedes around the Kincaid mansion to the carriage house in the back, he couldn't help but smile. After having lunch with Lily, she had asked him to stay for a bit so they could talk, but he'd had to decline because of an afternoon meeting with the president of the dockworkers' union. He had, however, managed to convince her to let him pick her up after the meeting for a trip to check out the most recently renovated exhibit at the aquarium, then have an early dinner at the little bistro she loved in the French Quarter. As far as he was concerned, that was progress in getting things back to the way they had been before his mother's dinner party.

Parking the car, he hesitated before opening the driver's door. Everything had been going great between them until the night of the party. But immediately afterward, Lily had decided to be conveniently busy whenever he asked her out. Could his mother have possibly said something to Lily that evening, causing her to have a sudden change of heart about seeing him? Or had the thirteen-year difference in their ages suddenly become a problem for her?

He dismissed the latter thought outright. Surely he would have had an indication if age had become an issue. They both enjoyed most of the same things and there had never been any sort of gap in conversation when they discussed the kind of music they liked to listen to, the books they had read or type of movies they preferred. No, the problem had to have been generated by his mother. He narrowed his eyes. It wouldn't surprise him if she had said something to insult or hurt Lily. In the past, when Charlotte Addison felt that someone was beneath her, she had never hesitated to let that person know all about just who she was in the pecking order of society. On more than one occasion, he had witnessed her boasting about her family pedigree and the fact that the Beauchamps were considered to be in the highest echelon of Charleston's social order.

But when could she have had the chance that evening to talk to Lily alone? He had purposely tried to keep

Lily at his side throughout the evening, anticipating that his mother might say something insulting. And he had been certain that given the chance, she would. Not only was The Kincaid Group the chief rival of Addison Industries, his mother seemed to have a huge problem with Reginald Kincaid in particular.

As he got out of the car and walked toward Lily's door, Daniel decided that by dinner he fully intended to have his questions answered and things straightened out between them. Then at his earliest possible convenience, he would confront his mother and firmly suggest that she mind her own business and stop meddling in his social life.

"I see you're ready to go," Daniel said when Lily stepped out of the carriage house before he reached the door.

"Actually, I had just returned from checking on my mother to see how she's doing when I heard you arrive," Lily said as she walked toward his car.

"How is your mother faring?" he asked, knowing the entire family had been dealing with one shock after another since their ordeal began.

"Momma is holding up surprisingly well," Lily said, frowning. "It makes me wonder if she might not be in a state of shock and everything that's happened will come crashing down on top of her later."

Opening the passenger door, Daniel helped her into the car, then walked around to slide into the driver's seat. "Sometimes grief brings out a strength in people they never knew they had," he suggested, suspecting that might be the case. With a quiet grace about her, Elizabeth Kincaid had always impressed him as having the heart and soul of a steel magnolia lying just beneath the surface of her soft-spoken, genteel exterior.

"I think you might be right," Lily said. "It's like she's become the rock that the rest of us are leaning on."

Reaching over, he covered her hand with his. "And don't forget. I'm here for you too, sweetheart."

Lily gave him an odd look before she finally nodded. "Thank you, Daniel. I appreciate your compassion, but as I've told you, I'm going to be fine."

Neither had a lot to say on the drive to the aquarium and Daniel hoped that the exhibit he wanted to show her would help relieve some of her tension and stress. "When I heard the plans for renovating this area of the aquarium, I knew it was something you would enjoy," he said as he bought two cups of shrimp from Gilligan's Shrimp Shack not far from the entrance to the exhibit.

Lily eyed the two plastic feeding sticks the attendant handed him as they walked toward the Saltmarsh Aviary. "What are we supposed to do with those?"

"We're going to feed the stingrays," he said, anticipating her reaction. He wasn't disappointed when her eyes brightened with almost childlike excitement.

"I've always thought stingrays look so graceful as they swim," Lily said as they walked up to the enormous tank.

He placed a shrimp on the end of one of the sticks, and handed it to her. "Just stick it down into the water and wait."

As he watched, Lily did as he instructed and in no time a large ray glided up to the stick and ate the shrimp. "Oh, Daniel, this is definitely my new favorite thing about the aquarium."

Her enthusiasm was infectious and by the time both

shrimp cups were empty, Daniel felt as if he were a good ten years younger. It was always this way when he was with Lily. Her zest for life never failed to improve his mood and he found that his outlook wasn't nearly as jaded and cynical as it had been just a few hours ago.

"Thank you for bringing me," Lily said as they walked on to view the puffer fish and diamondback terrapins in the mock saltmarsh tidal creek.

He shook his head. "No, I'm the one who should be thanking you." Reaching down, he took her hand in his and brought it to his lips to kiss the back. "Seeing all this wouldn't have been nearly as much fun without you."

By the time they left the aquarium, Lily looked more relaxed and he gave himself a mental pat on the back for thinking to bring her to the exhibit. "What do you have planned for after dinner?" he asked on the short drive to her favorite bistro.

For the second time that afternoon, she gave him a look as if trying to decide what she wanted to say. "Mr. Parsons stopped by my mother's this morning to drop off the keys to the different properties my father left to me and my siblings. I thought I would go take a look at the home I inherited."

"Where's it located?"

"In the Battery."

"Nice area," he said, meaning it. He had been raised in the Battery, and it was where some of the finest homes in Charleston were located. Steering the car into the restaurant's parking lot, he switched off the engine and turned to face her. "Since we're already out, why don't I drive you over there after we eat?"

She gave him that look again—the one she had been

giving him all afternoon. If he didn't know better, he would swear she suspected him of something. But he didn't have a clue what he could have done to deserve it.

"That might be a good idea," she finally said. "I think I'd like to get your opinion on what I should do with the place."

As he guided her into the bistro, Daniel grinned. "If you want to know how to pack it, ship it or liquidate it, I'm your guy. Decorating? Not so much."

After a scrumptious dinner, Daniel drove along South Battery Street toward the Beauchamp mansion, and Lily couldn't help but feel a bit apprehensive about touring the house with him. She purposely hadn't told him that the home she inherited was once owned by his mother—the very house that was supposed to one day be his. She wasn't sure why she had omitted the information, other than she had a feeling his immediate reaction when he saw the place would tell her if he was interested in getting it back or really didn't care about it.

"That's it," she said, pointing to the stately home up ahead.

"You inherited Colonel Sam's old place?" Daniel asked, clearly astounded. "Up until fifteen years ago, this used to belong to my mother."

His surprise was genuine and Lily was almost certain that Daniel was unaware her father had bought the home. "I've always thought it was one of the most beautiful mansions in the Battery," she said, smiling.

He shrugged as he turned the car into the driveway. "I guess it's all right."

"Don't you like historic homes?" she asked, wondering how anyone could resist the charm and beauty of antebellum architecture.

"I think they're great when someone takes the time to keep them up," he answered, getting out of the car. When he came around to open her door for her, he added, "It's when they're allowed to fall into a state of disrepair that they look like any other old house that's been let go."

"The outside looks as if someone has been taking good care of this one," she said, crossing her fingers that the inside looked just as nice.

"I hope for your sake they have," he said, guiding her up the steps onto the piazza. "The last time I was in this place it was in need of some serious renovations and looked to me like it could turn into a bottomless money pit."

Reaching into her handbag, Lily removed the set of keys Mr. Parsons had tagged as belonging to the house. "I hope the electricity is on. Otherwise, I'll have to come back tomorrow in the daylight to see what needs to be done."

Daniel took the keys from her and, unlocking the door, stepped inside ahead of her. "Let me find the switch and we'll see if the lights work."

When the foyer's crystal chandelier sparkled to life, Lily crossed the threshold and felt as if she had indeed entered the princess's castle. Apparently her father had seen to it that the mansion had been completely restored to its original grandeur.

"This is everything I thought it would be and more," Lily said, in awe of her surroundings.

The walls, wainscoting and ornate dentiled ceiling cornice had been painted a rich cream that glowed warmly in the chandelier's light and contrasted perfectly with the highly polished heart-pine floor. A graceful sweeping staircase with a black cypress banister and steps ascended to the upper floors and Lily could only imagine how beautiful the rest of the house had to be.

"Wow," Daniel said, looking around. "I'm impressed. Your dad spent a small fortune to bring this old place back to life. I've never seen it look this good."

"I can't believe it's mine," Lily said, falling in love with the house all over again.

"Let's check out the rest of it," he said, taking her by the hand.

As he led her through the mansion, Lily marveled at the attention that had been paid to detail. Every room was fully furnished and although the furniture was new, it had been chosen to complement the antebellum style, while still projecting a comfortable homey atmosphere.

Whoever designed the master suite had pulled out all the stops to make it the most luxurious room in the house. From the balcony off the sitting room overlooking the courtyard below, to the his-and-her bathrooms, the interior designer had outdone himself.

By the time she and Daniel had toured all the rooms and walked out onto the lighted terrace, Lily had to ask, "How could your mother part with such a beautiful place?"

"It didn't look anything like this when she owned it and besides, she really didn't have a choice." Putting his arm around her shoulders, he led her across the yard toward the carriage house. "Right after I graduated from college, my dad died and I had to take over Addison Industries. That's when we discovered that he wasn't the best of managers. The business was in such bad shape financially, it took her selling off the summer home on Hilton Head Island, as well as parting with this place, just for her to survive until I could get the business back in the black and out of the danger of bankruptcy."

"I'm so sorry, Daniel." Lily couldn't begin to imagine how stressful the situation had to have been for him. "You've done an amazing job of bringing it back. I've heard RJ and my father talk about Addison Industries being TKG's toughest competitor."

He shrugged. "It wasn't easy, but I think it was harder on my mom than anyone else. For the first time in her life, she had to adhere to a strict budget and she was scared to death that some of her snooty friends would find out that she was on the verge of being destitute."

Lily couldn't help but wonder how Charlotte Addison's pride had survived such a devastating blow. "Did you know she had sold the home to my father?"

"I had my hands full with getting Addison Industries back on its feet," he said, shaking his head. "I didn't have time, nor did I care what she did with this place, just as long as I didn't have to deal with it." His adamant tone convinced Lily that Daniel truly had no idea who had bought the mansion or that he had any interest in getting it back.

As he started to unlock the door to the carriage house, she turned and, rising on tiptoe, impulsively kissed his cheek.

"What was that for?" he asked, chuckling as he turned and wrapped her in his arms.

"I'm just happy," she said, not wanting to explain about her unfounded suspicions. "Do you mind?"

"You're not going to get any complaints out of me," he said, using his index finger to trace her jawline.

His gentle touch reminded her of how tender he could be, how much care he took when he made love to her. "Daniel, I'm not certain—"

"I'll be sure for both of us," he said, lowering his head to brush her lips with his.

When his mouth settled over hers, Lily brought her hands up to his chest to push away from him, to put distance between herself and the temptation he posed. The issue of how much he knew about her father buying the house had been settled, but she had yet to tell him the news that would no doubt put a permanent end to his attraction to her.

But as his arms tightened around her and he traced her lips with his tongue, she abandoned all thought and allowed him to kiss her the way she had wanted him to do the night before. There would be plenty of time within the next few days to tell him about the baby and face the future without Daniel in her life.

As he explored her with a thoroughness that threatened to turn her insides to warm pudding, a tingling sensation began to spread throughout her body and she welcomed his deepening of the kiss. It had been the better part of three weeks since he had held her like this, made her feel as if she was the most cherished creature on earth. And heaven help her, she didn't want him to stop.

He pulled her closer and the feel of his hard, muscular body pressed to hers sent a flash of heat racing from the top of her head to the soles of her feet. His chest muscles beneath her hands flexed as she clutched his shirt and she could feel his heart pounding against her fingertips.

"I've missed you, sweetheart," he said, easing away from the kiss. "I've missed holding you like this."

"Me, too."

Lily could have denied that she had missed him, but what was the point? Her response to him had been every bit as eager as it had always been and there was no sense in her lying to either one of them.

"What happened, Lily?" he whispered close to her ear. "Why did you stop seeing me?"

"Please, not now," she begged, not wanting reality to intrude. She kissed the exposed skin at his open collar. "Could we please leave this for another time?"

Just when she thought he was going to press the issue, he leaned back and, staring down into her eyes for several long moments, finally nodded. "It can wait for now." He gave her a smile that made her feel warm all over. "Why don't we check out the carriage house, then lock up and go back to your place."

"It sounds like we have a plan, Mr. Addison," she agreed. "You can drop me off and then go home."

He gave her an exasperated look, but didn't comment.

She knew he was confused by her insistence that she wanted to be left alone, then her allowing him to hold her, kiss her. But she was doing her best to distance herself from him and if he wasn't such a source of temptation for her, she would be able to do that. Unfortunately, from the moment he took her into his arms at the Autumn Ball, she had discovered a weakness within herself that she hadn't known existed. Whenever Daniel touched her, she seemed to lose a will of her own. It was something she needed to work on—had to work on—or risk losing her sanity when he found out about the baby and lost interest in her.

When they entered the carriage house, they found that her father had turned it into a studio with huge floor-to-ceiling windows to let in plenty of natural light. "It looks like your dad had planned on an artist using this," Daniel said, giving her a knowing wink as they looked around the spacious work area.

Lily had a hard time blinking back her tears. It was clear her father had her in mind when he'd commissioned the renovations of the property, meaning that he had planned for some time to make her childhood dream of living here come true.

"When I was a little girl, Daddy used to take me to White Point Gardens across the street. We would sit for hours on one of the benches staring at this place and I would tell him stories I made up about the princess who lived here."

"I'll bet she had red hair and blue eyes," Daniel teased, walking up behind her to put his arms around her.

She nodded as she indulged herself just one more time and leaned back against him. "The princess would stand in the cupola and look out at Charleston Harbor."

"What was she looking for?" His deep baritone vibrated against her back and caused a delightful fluttering in her lower belly.

"She was watching for her prince to sail into Charleston Harbor and come home to live with her in the castle," Lily answered.

"Of course," he murmured close to her ear. "Any princess worth her salt always waits for her prince, whether he's sailing up in a ship or riding a big white horse."

"Now you're making fun of me," she said, smiling as she turned in his arms to face him.

"Maybe just a little," he said, grinning. "Have you ever thought of writing children's books, instead of just illustrating them?"

"My father always thought I should," she said, doing her best to stifle a yawn. She had missed the afternoon nap that she had been taking since becoming pregnant. "But since college, the major children's publishers have kept me so busy illustrating for others, I haven't had time to think much about it."

"You should," he said, kissing her forehead. "Now, why don't I walk you to my car and then I'll go back and lock up. You're starting to look pretty tired."

She nodded as they left the carriage house. "It has been a long day."

While Lily waited in the car for Daniel to return from turning off lights and locking the house, she couldn't help but think about what her father had said in his letter. She was a strong, capable woman who he was confident would make the right decision about the mansion. He hadn't insisted that she keep the property, but he had everything in place for her, anticipating that she would want to.

Staring up at the stately home, she knew it was foolish for one person to even contemplate living alone in a house with more than ten thousand square feet of living space. But her father had spared no expense in getting it ready for her. He had given her her dream and, wise or not, she was going to take it.

"I've made a decision about what I'm going to do with the mansion," Lily said when Daniel returned to the car.

"And just what might that be?" he asked, starting the car and driving it down the driveway to the street.

"It's going to take me a week or so to make arrangements, but as soon as I can get things packed up, I'm going to move in and live here."

Four

For the next week after touring the mansion with Lily, Daniel found himself embroiled in a labor dispute with the dockworkers that left little time for anything but a few hurried phone calls and a standing order at the local florist for a daily bouquet of flowers to be delivered to her apartment. Lily hadn't asked him to stop calling and seemed to appreciate all of the flowers, but they still weren't completely back to where they had been with their affair before Christmas. That was the first thing he intended to remedy as soon as possible.

It would already have been taken care of by now, if not for the snag that had developed with the labor force. He had thought he and the union president had worked things out the day he had taken Lily to the aquarium, but apparently the rank and file had other ideas. Just that afternoon, he had been able to come to an agreement with the dockworkers and anticipated being able to spend a lot more time with her.

Unfortunately, tonight was not one of those times. In one of their phone conversations, Lily had explained that she would be babysitting her nephew on Thursday evenings for the next few weeks, while her brothers worked on getting reports ready for Jack Sinclair. So what was he going to do with his evening?

As he sat at his desk contemplating his options, his cell phone rang. "Daniel Addison," he said, answering the call.

"Daniel, I'm so glad I caught you."

"Hello, Charlotte." At her request, he hadn't called her "Mom" or "Mother" in years.

"I haven't talked to you since Christmas Day and I was wondering when I may expect a visit," she said in her usual formal tone.

"I'm free this evening," he answered, deciding not to put her off. He did want to talk to his mother about the night of the dinner party and what she might have said to Lily. This evening seemed as good a time as any to do that.

"I think that would be marvelous, Daniel. Shall I have Cook set an extra place for dinner?" she asked.

Barely able to keep from rolling his eyes at her pretentiousness, he sighed heavily. "Sure, why not."

"I'll expect you at six then." His mother ended the call as she always did, without saying goodbye.

Twenty minutes later, as he drove to the home he had grown up in on East Battery Street, just half a mile from the Beauchamp mansion, Daniel couldn't help but think about how vastly different his childhood had been from Lily's. She had been raised in a loving home with several brothers and sisters, who remained quite close as adults.

He, on the other hand, had been the only child of a frequently aloof mother and a father who could only be described as a dreamer. To say his parents were a mismatched couple was an understatement and Daniel couldn't understand how they had managed to stay together for over twenty-five years of marriage.

Charlotte Beauchamp-Addison was all about maintaining her standing in society and feeling superior among her circle of so-called friends, while George Addison had drifted through life with a laid-back, "whatever will be, will be" attitude. Daniel sometimes even wondered if his father had purposely ignored the signs of an impending heart attack, in order to die and get away from the pretentiousness and snobbery of life with Charlotte.

When he parked his car, Daniel entered through the back door of the house. He had always liked coming in through the kitchen. At least he got a warm greeting from Rosemary, the housekeeper and cook who had worked for his parents for as long as he could remember. It hadn't been easy, but he had managed to see that the woman remained on the job, even through the times when he hadn't been sure he would be able to bring Addison Industries back to solvency. But the woman was, and always had been, considered part of the family.

"How's my favorite girl?" Daniel asked, smiling as he walked over to where the gray-haired woman stood, stirring something in a pot on the stove.

"I'm mad at you, Daniel Addison," she said, her attention never wavering from what she was cooking.

"You haven't been by to see me in almost three weeks. Do you know how hard it is for a woman my age not seeing the boy I helped raised? I could very well die of a broken heart."

Daniel chuckled as he kissed the woman's wrinkled cheek. "I'm sorry, Rosemary, but there's been a lot going on since Christmas. Will it make you feel better if I try to do better in the future?"

She turned to give him a sympathetic look. "I heard about Miss Lily's daddy. How is that poor child doing?"

"As well as can be expected under the circumstances," he answered. The woman had only met Lily once, at the dinner party before the holidays, but she and Lily had hit it off right away.

"My heart goes out to that girl, losing him the way she did," Rosemary said, her kind brown eyes shining with unshed tears. "You be sure to tell her that I've got her and her family in my thoughts and prayers."

"I'll do that," he said, knowing the kind-hearted woman his mother insisted on calling "Cook" was completely sincere with her sympathy.

Continuing into the sitting room, he found Charlotte posed by the window, staring out at Charleston Harbor. It was her favorite place to be when receiving guests.

"I don't know why you insist on coming in the back way like a common servant, Daniel," she admonished, turning to face him.

"Hello to you too, Charlotte," he said, sitting down in one of the chairs by the fireplace. "How have you been?"

His question was all it took to get his mother started on the various charity functions she was helping to plan and the latest gossip circulating through the garden club. Barely listening, something she said suddenly caught his attention.

"What was that?" he asked, sitting up straight in the chair.

"I said that Madelyn Worthington told me all about poor Elizabeth Kincaid's betrayal by that wretched man," Charlotte said, patting an imaginary out-of-place hair back into place. "I've known for years that Reginald Kincaid was nothing but a low-bred scoundrel and I'm not the least bit surprised he turned out to be such an embarrassment to his family. Having a mistress and two bastard children in Greenville is just a disgrace."

"Only one of the woman's sons belongs to Kincaid," he corrected. "And when did you start feeling sorry for Elizabeth Kincaid?" He distinctly remembered Charlotte referring to the woman as being a fool for marrying beneath her station.

His mother ignored the question, asking one of her own. "Are you still keeping company with that youngest Kincaid girl?"

"As a matter of fact, I am," he said proudly.

Charlotte looked anything but pleased. "Really? I thought the two of you had a parting of the ways just before Christmas."

Daniel narrowed his eyes. Now he knew his mother had something to do with his and Lily's breakup. Otherwise, how would she have known?

"We stopped seeing each other for a few weeks, but just recently started dating again." Technically they had only gone out once since running into each other at the lawyer's office, but he fully intended for their trip to the aquarium to be the first of many outings they shared. "Why do you ask?"

"Oh, the night of my dinner party it seemed like she was losing interest in continuing your association," his mother said calmly.

With years of practice at being a master manipulator, he wasn't fooled by Charlotte's disinterested demeanor. His mother knew a lot more about why Lily tried to end their affair than he did and he intended to find out what that was.

"What did you say to her?" he asked. "And don't tell me you don't know what I'm talking about, Charlotte. I know exactly how you operate."

She didn't so much as flinch at his accusation. "I just pointed out that since your divorce, you've made it no secret that you aren't interested in anything long-term with a woman or marrying to carry on the family name." Her smug smile caused him to clench his back teeth together so hard, he was surprised it didn't break his jaw. "She comes from a large family and I'm sure that she has ideas of raising a brood of her own one day. It's better that she knows now that isn't what you're interested in than to give her false hope for the future. Besides, she doesn't have the breeding of a young woman suited for a man with your standing in the community."

"And I guess Charisma did?" Daniel retorted.

"I'll admit that Charisma was a bit high-strung, but you can't deny she had a suitable background," Charlotte answered as if the issue was as important to him as it was to her. "Her family has been a part of Charleston society almost as long as the Beauchamps and Addisons. She would have passed along the traits you would want in an offspring."

"I shouldn't be surprised that you thought she was good wife material," he said, unable to keep the bitter tone from his voice. "She's just like you, and I think that the traits you seem to think are so important would be better off not polluting the next generation."

"Charisma is like me, isn't she?" Charlotte said, smiling as if he had paid her a compliment and completely ignoring his disdain for the qualities her grandchild might inherit. She shook her head. "She was my best hope for a grandchild to carry on the family's esteemed name."

"Yeah, the two of you were as alike as I've ever seen—sweet as honey when things are going your way, but when they aren't, you turn as vicious as a shark in a feeding frenzy." He shook his head. "If I had wanted to carry on the family name, it certainly wouldn't have been with Charisma."

"Then why did you bother marrying her in the first place?" Charlotte asked, raising one darkly penciled eyebrow.

"Because, like you, she only showed the side of herself that she wanted me to see until she got her hooks in me," he said, disgusted with himself for not seeing through his ex-wife's facade sooner. "By the time she showed her true colors, it was too late. We had already walked down the aisle."

"But you must have cared for her at some point," his mother persisted. "The two of you were married for almost three years."

"I tried to make things work, but I'm not like my father," he stated flatly. "I finally faced the reality of the situation and realized that no matter what I did or how I did it, it was never going to keep her from making my life a living hell. I chose the peace and freedom of being single over a life of the abject misery Dad suffered."

"Your father needed a strong woman to guide him," Charlotte said, unabashed by her son's observations.

"Well, I don't." He glared at his mother. "I prefer a woman to be my equal, not one who tells me every move to make and how to make it."

"Do you honestly believe that Kincaid girl is your equal?" Charlotte scoffed.

"Yes, I do. But that is absolutely none of your concern." Daniel had heard enough and he didn't think he could stomach much more of his mother's arrogance. "I think I'll take a rain check on that dinner, Charlotte." He rose to leave. "And I'm giving you fair warning. In the future, you would do well to keep your nose out of my business and your opinions to yourself. I'll see who the hell I want for as long as I want and I don't intend to listen to another word about it from you."

Without waiting for his mother's reaction, he walked out of the room. On his way through the kitchen, he apologized to Rosemary for skipping her delicious meal, then headed home to the peace and quiet of his condo. Eating alone was preferable to listening to Charlotte extol the virtues of his cold, intractable ex-wife's pedigree, while running down a warm, caring woman like Lily.

To keep from saying anything against his mother, Lily had simply stopped seeing him rather than cause a rift between them. That was the kind of class and breeding Charlotte should applaud and strive for—not run down.

Lily Kincaid was twice the woman his mother or his ex-wife would ever be and if he hadn't known that before, he certainly did now.

* * *

"Are you sure that living in that huge house all by yourself is what you really want?" Kara asked, clearly worried.

"Yes." Lily knew her sister was voicing the concern of her entire family when she stopped by to pick up some extra rolls of Bubble Wrap Kara kept at her shop. "I've always loved that house and now that I've seen the inside, I can't think of anywhere else I'd rather live."

"I haven't driven up to Hilton Head to see about my property yet," Kara said, handing Lily a box filled with several rolls of the packing material. "I've been so busy trying to get everything ready for Laurel and Eli's wedding, I just haven't had the time."

"Has Laurel chosen the colors she wants to use for the wedding and reception?" Lily asked, hoping her sister chose a shade for the bridesmaids' dresses that didn't clash with red hair.

"She's leaving it up to me and Eli to decide." Kara shook her head. "I don't think I've ever had a bride who didn't care what color scheme was used at her wedding or who encouraged the groom to help the planner make all the choices for her."

"Well, she is rather busy now that she's handling the press releases for the family, as well as public relations for TKG," Lily said, wondering if that was all there was to Laurel's disinterest. At times it seemed that Kara was more excited about their sister's wedding to Eli Houghton, owner of a luxury resort on Seabrook Island in the Outer Banks, than Laurel was.

"I'm sure that her hands are full," Kara agreed. "But still—" When the phone rang, she stopped and held up her finger as she picked it up. "Prestige Events, may I put you on hold for just a moment?"

"I'll let you get back to work," Lily said, smiling when her sister muted the call. "My dishes and I thank you for the Bubble Wrap."

"If you need more packing materials or someone to help you move, just let me know," Kara said, already pressing the button to return to the call.

As Lily drove back to the carriage house from Kara's shop, she went through a mental checklist of all that she wanted to accomplish for the day. She needed to sketch out a few more scenes for the new children's book she was illustrating and pack more of her things for her move to the Beauchamp mansion. And, of course, somewhere between drawing a mouse wearing a fedora and wrapping china with Bubble Wrap, she would need to take a nap.

She smiled as she turned into the driveway leading back to the carriage house. Once filled with almost boundless energy, since becoming pregnant she required a nap around the same time every afternoon. The doctor had told her that the fatigue was common and would probably disappear after the first trimester only to return during the last few weeks before giving birth. But as out of character as it was for her to sleep during the day, she fully intended to enjoy every minute of her pregnancy even if she had to do it without the baby's father.

Thinking about Daniel, she sighed wistfully. She hadn't seen him for the past week, and whether it was smart or not, she had missed him. He had called her as often as he could and sent flowers every day, but it wasn't the same as being with him. And that was dangerous to her peace of mind.

She wished things could be different—that he wanted what she wanted. But he didn't, and all the wishing in the world wasn't going to change that. She was going to have to tell him about the baby, and as soon as she got moved into the Beauchamp House, that was exactly what she was going to do.

When she drove around her parents' home to the carriage house in back, she found Daniel waiting for her. Parking her Mini Cooper next to his white Mercedes, her heart sped up. "Speak of the devil," she murmured.

"Don't you have to work today?" she asked as they both got out of their cars. Opening the back of the Mini to remove the box of Bubble Wrap, she started toward the front door. "I thought you had another meeting with the dockworkers."

"It was canceled," he said, walking over to take the box from her. "We were able to get things resolved late yesterday afternoon."

"It must be a relief to have that over with." She knew from listening to her father and brothers how disruptive the labor force walking off the job could be to an international shipping company.

"But don't you have other duties to attend to as CEO of Addison Industries?" she asked, not at all pleased with herself for being so happy to see him.

The trip to the aquarium and the kiss they shared at the mansion were wonderful, but they changed nothing. He was still a man who was completely turned off by commitment and having children. And she still wanted the happily-ever-after—a loving husband, marriage and a big family.

But it was going to be a serious test of her will-power not to fall for him all over again. He just looked so darned good. In a suit and tie, he was drop-dead gorgeous. Daniel Addison wearing blue jeans, a black T-shirt and a brown leather blazer was positively devastating. It was all she could do to keep from abandoning her resolve and throwing herself into his arms.

"That's the beauty of being the boss," Daniel said, oblivious to her inner struggle. Easily handling the lightweight box with one arm, he held up a sack from a nearby Chinese restaurant with the other. "I can take off for an early start to the weekend whenever I want to."

Opening her front door, Lily led the way into the apartment, then took the box of Bubble Wrap from him. "As you can see, everything is in a state of total chaos right now," she said, finding an empty place next to a bouquet of flowers on the coffee table to set the box.

"I see you have quite a few things packed." She watched him look around at the cartons and boxes already sealed and stacked for the move. "You aren't taking the furniture, are you?"

Lily shook her head. "Since Daddy had the mansion fully furnished, there wouldn't be anywhere to put any of it." She threaded her way around a pile of empty containers to the dining table on the far side of the room. "I thought I would leave my furniture here in case Momma wants to let one of the servants move in or if she decides to rent it out to someone."

He set the sack of takeout on the table. "When do you plan on moving?"

"Over the next three days." She walked into the kitchen to get a couple of disposable plates and plastic cutlery. "I thought I would take the lighter boxes over there tomorrow and Sunday. Then, when the movers get the heavier things on Monday, all that should be left to do is find where I want to put things at the mansion."

"I have an idea," he said, taking food from the sack. "Why don't we move some of this over there this afternoon. Since I'm off for the rest of the day, I can carry boxes inside while you start putting things away."

Lily nibbled on her lower lip as she thought about his offer. "It would be nice if some of this mess was cleared out of the way."

Daniel looked over at the tall stack of moving cartons in the living room. "I'm going to go so far as to say it would be a hell of a lot less dangerous, too."

"It is going to take several trips," she thought aloud as they sat down to eat. "My little car can only hold so much, even with the backseats folded down, and I'll probably need the extra afternoon to get everything moved."

"Do you actually enjoy driving that little toy?" Daniel asked, handing her a carton of sweet-and-sour chicken.

"You sound just like my brother," she said, frowning. "RJ keeps telling me I should replace it with a real car."

He raised one eyebrow. "I take it that isn't something you want to do?"

"I love my Mini Cooper," she said, defending her little car. "I could easily afford to replace it with a larger, more expensive model, but I don't want to. It's fun to drive and I think it suits my personality."

"Okay," Daniel said slowly, as if knowing he was treading on a sensitive subject. "We'll use it and my car this afternoon, then tomorrow I'll get one of my company pickup trucks to move what's left."

Having his help would greatly cut down on the amount of time it took her to move. But the more she was with Daniel, the bigger threat he posed to her peace of mind. If she continued to be around him, there was a very real danger of her falling for him again, and it would make things that much harder for her when she told him about the baby and he walked out of her life for good.

"I can't ask you to do that," she said regretfully. "I'm sure you have other things you need to be doing."

"Nope. And besides, you didn't ask." Reaching across the table, he covered her hand with his, sending a tingling awareness spiraling throughout her body. "I wouldn't have offered if I didn't want to help, sweetheart."

"I don't want—"

"Just say yes, Lily," he commanded with the same smile that never failed to make her heart skip a beat.

Lily stared at him for a few seconds longer as she began to realize that she had already lost the battle she had been waging within herself. Sighing, she gave in to what they both wanted. "All right. Yes, you can help me move."

Daniel carried the last box of art supplies into the studio in the Beauchamp carriage house just as daylight was starting to fade to dusk. He and Lily had made several trips from her parents' place over to the mansion and reduced the amount of boxes piled in her living room to just a few. They had even managed to move most of her clothes and toiletries.

"It shouldn't take long to move the rest of your things tomorrow," he said, watching her lay out drawings of a mouse wearing a trench coat and fedora across her worktable. "We'll be able to move twice as many boxes with the truck. You'll probably even be able to cancel the movers for Monday."

"Thank you for all the help, Daniel. I really appreciate it." When she looked up, her vivid blue eyes brightened and he could practically see the wheels turning in her pretty head. "If I wanted to, I could even start staying here tonight."

"You could," he said, nodding. "But by the time we have dinner and you got back over here, it would be time for bed. Wouldn't it be better to get a good night's sleep at the apartment, then you'll already be there to finish the move when I come by tomorrow morning with the truck."

"I suppose you're right," she said, putting the last of her drawing pencils into a holder on the worktable.

Wrapping his arms around her, he pulled her to him. "Why don't we go back to your place, have a pizza delivered and open a bottle of wine to celebrate your move."

"That sounds nice, but I think I'll pass on the wine," she said, resting her head against his chest. She was too tired to pull away and besides, it felt good to be in his arms. "I think I'd rather have the pizza and then a big bowl of ice cream with lots of chocolate syrup and peanut butter mixed in with it for dessert."

He leaned back to see the expression on her face. "You're serious?"

"Absolutely," she said, grinning. "I've had ice cream,

chocolate and peanut butter almost every night for the past few weeks."

"Really?"

She nodded. "Why do you think I keep that large carton of vanilla ice cream in the freezer?"

"Okay, I'll give it a try. We'll have ice cream to celebrate," he said, laughing. He kissed her forehead. "Then I'll run an extra couple of miles tomorrow morning just to work it off."

Ten minutes later as they turned the corner onto the street where the Kincaid home was located, Daniel slowed the car to a stop and swore under his breath at the sight a couple of blocks ahead. "What the hell's going on?"

Lily gasped. "Are all those vans and cars parked in front of my mother's house?"

"It looks that way," he said, deciding to drive on past the media circus. "Why don't you call to see what's up before we try to get past them to your apartment."

"I'm almost afraid to." When she took her cell phone from her purse, he noticed that her hands were shaking. "I'm not sure I want to know."

He could understand her apprehension. Although he hadn't been with her when the family had been notified of her father's death, Daniel had seen the news-footage reporting from in front of the Kincaid mansion. He imagined it had to have been something like the scene up ahead of them.

"The line is busy. I'll try RJ's number," she said as they sped past the reporters and cameramen from all the area television stations. "RJ, what on earth is going on at Momma's?" she asked when her brother answered.

Daniel had a gut feeling that whatever was going on, it wasn't going to be good news.

"Oh, my God! You can't be serious."

One glance at Lily and Daniel steered the car over to the curb. Her peaches-and-cream complexion had bleached to a ghostly white and her eyes were bright with tears.

Looking over at him, she nodded. "Yes, I'm with Daniel. We moved most of my things to the mansion this afternoon." She paused. "Yes, of course. I'm sure I'll be fine at the Beauchamp house tonight. Do you think the media will be gone by morning?" She paused for her brother's answer, then added, "I promise I'll wait for you to call tomorrow before I try to go back to the carriage house."

"What's happened?" Daniel asked when she ended the call.

"The police just released a report stating that my father's death has been ruled a…homicide," she said, the single word catching on a sob. "RJ strongly suggested that I stay at the Beauchamp house tonight if I want to avoid being accosted by the media when I try to get back home."

"You could stay at my place," Daniel offered.

"I'd rather not," she said, shaking her head. "It wasn't a secret that we were seeing each other before Christmas and I'm not entirely certain some photographer trying to get a story won't be lurking in the shadows."

What she said made sense. They had been featured on the society page of the newspaper more times than he cared to count during their three-month affair, and with the breaking news that Reginald Kincaid had been murdered, there was a very real possibility that his condo would be on the media's radar as well.

"I'm staying with you," Daniel said, steering the car back onto the street. "I don't want you being alone until things quiet down."

"I'll b-be okay," she said through chattering teeth that had nothing to do with the mild winter temperature. "I don't w-want—"

"This isn't negotiable," he said firmly. "If you're concerned about the sleeping arrangements, don't be. I understand that things between us moved a bit fast when we first started seeing each other. We haven't been intimate for several weeks and you're not ready to make love with me again. I get that. But there are five guest bedrooms in that house and I'm sure I can find a comfortable place to sleep."

When she fell silent, he took that as a yes, and after a quick detour to his condo for a change of clothes, Daniel drove them back to the Battery and, parking at the rear entrance of the house, used Lily's key to let them in the back door. He didn't want to use the front entrance for obvious reasons. It wasn't common knowledge that Lily had inherited the mansion, but he wasn't going to take any chances that a stray member of the paparazzi had recognized his car when they drove past her mother's place and followed them.

As soon as he had the door secured behind them and the alarm system turned on, Daniel took Lily into his arms. "I'm so sorry all this is happening, sweetheart. If I could make it all go away, I would."

"I can't believe someone…murdered my father," she said, wrapping her arms around his waist as if he was a lifeline. "Who would do that? Why would they do that?"

"I don't know." He held her close. "But I'm sure the authorities will find whoever it is and bring them to justice."

"I hope so," she said, trembling against him. "RJ said that after the police interview the security team at TKG and get preliminary results from the autopsy, they're going to interview each member of the family. Does that mean we're all under suspicion?"

Daniel didn't want to tell her that was most likely the case. She'd had enough upset and he wasn't going to cause her more by confirming her assumption.

Thinking quickly, he shook his head. "It's probably just a matter of investigative procedure. There might be something that you or one of your siblings could tell the detectives that would give them a lead to follow or a clue who the killer might be."

"I suppose you're right," she said, sounding emotionally spent.

"One of those boxes we brought over contained towels, didn't it?" he asked. When she nodded, he guided her toward the back stairs, leading from the kitchen to the second floor. "Let's go upstairs and get you into a warm bath. Maybe it will relieve some of the tension and help you sleep."

While Lily took a nice soaking bath in one of the two master bathrooms, Daniel took a quick shower in the other. As he toweled himself dry, he wondered who could have killed Reginald Kincaid and why.

It was a fact of life that men in high corporate positions weren't without their share of enemies. Whether it was a disgruntled employee, a business rival or a radical member of a special interest group, there was always someone who didn't agree with the way a CEO conducted business and the decisions he had to make for the welfare of the company. But who would have taken their grievance to the extreme and resorted to murder?

Pulling on a pair of boxer briefs, Daniel walked into the bedroom and sat on the edge of the king-size bed as he waited for Lily to finish her bath. He didn't like that she was having to relive the loss of her father. She had just started to adjust to losing the man and now the uncertainty of what had happened, and why, was starting all over again.

But he liked even less that there was an unknown murderer on the loose and there was no way of knowing if he intended to target another member of the Kincaid family.

Five

When Lily came out of the bathroom, she stopped short at the sight of Daniel sitting on the edge of the bed wearing nothing but a pair of dark blue boxer briefs. She had seen his body many times during their three-month affair and it never failed to cause her pulse to race. But tonight? With learning that her father had been murdered and seeing reporters camped in front of her mother's house, how could she possibly be distracted by how sexy he looked?

But that was exactly what she was thinking. With broad muscular shoulders, well-developed pectoral muscles and enough ripples on his abdomen to make a bodybuilder proud, Daniel Addison exuded over six feet of pure sex appeal.

"Feeling more relaxed?" he asked as she walked over to the side of the bed.

"A little," she said, wishing that she could close her eyes and things would be the way they were before his mother's dinner party. Her father would still be alive and she wouldn't be getting ready to have the talk that she knew would send Daniel running in the opposite direction from her. But then, that would mean she wasn't pregnant. And no matter how strained things became between them when she told him about the baby, her pregnancy was something she wouldn't wish away for anything in the world.

Rising to his feet, he walked around to where she stood and pulled her to him. "I'm sure things will look a little brighter in the morning when you're more rested."

"Daniel, there's something we need to discuss," she said, loving the feel of his bare chest pressed to her cheek. She had put off telling him long enough. He might not want a child but he was going to have one, and it was past time that she told him about the baby. "It's really important."

"Not tonight." He shook his head and, reaching down, pulled the comforter back for her to get into bed. "You need sleep and there's nothing that can't wait until tomorrow."

"But if I don't tell you now, I might not—"

He put his index finger to her lips to stop her. "Whatever it is, you can tell me in the morning."

Too tired to argue, she simply nodded and climbed into bed. Daniel was right. Her news had waited this long, it could wait another eight hours.

"I'll be on the couch in the sitting room if you need me," he said, pulling the comforter over her.

"I thought you were going to sleep down the hall in

one of the other bedrooms," she said, unable to stifle a yawn.

Leaning down, he gave her a quick kiss. "I decided that was too far away. Now try to get some rest, sweetheart."

As she watched him walk through the open French doors and into the sitting room, she couldn't help but feel disappointed that he had stuck to his word about sleeping in another room. She shouldn't be, she told herself, rolling to her side. Being held by him throughout the night, even if they didn't make love, would only complicate things and make it that much harder for her when they finally did discuss her pregnancy tomorrow morning.

Unable to stop thinking about how she should tell him that he was going to be a daddy in seven months, she must have drifted off to sleep. The next thing she knew, Daniel was stretching out on the bed beside her and gathering her into his arms.

"It's all right, Lily," he said, cradling her to his bare chest. He wiped the tears from her cheeks with the pad of his thumb. "I'm here, sweetheart. Everything is going to be fine. It was just a nightmare."

Leaning back to look at him, she couldn't tell him that it might have been a bad dream, but it was one that she feared would turn out to be all too prophetic. In the dream, she had told him about the baby and watched the attraction in his eyes turn to utter contempt.

When she had ended their affair, she might have told herself that she was calling a halt to things before she got in too deep and suffered a broken heart when he lost interest in seeing her after learning about the baby. But the truth of the matter was, she had already fallen in love with Daniel, had most likely loved him from the moment they met.

She knew it was foolish and that she would suffer more emotional pain when he learned her secret and severed all ties with her, but she couldn't resist wanting one more night in his arms. Snuggling against his solid strength, she asked, "Will you please keep holding me, Daniel?"

"I'm not going anywhere, sweetheart," he promised as he ran his hands up and down her back. "Not until you tell me to."

Lily rested her head on his shoulder and her hand on his broad chest. With the steady beat of his heart beneath her palm and his strong arms wrapped around her, she felt more content, more secure than she had in several weeks. It felt as if in his arms was where she belonged, where she would always belong.

"Lily, don't get me wrong," he said, his voice a bit rusty. "I love the way your hand feels on my body. But if you keep that up, I can't guarantee that I'll be able to continue being a gentleman for much longer."

Realizing that she had been moving her fingers over his pectoral muscles and the upper part of his abdomen, she stopped immediately. "I'm sorry. I didn't realize…"

When she started to pull her hand away, he covered it with his and, holding it to him, gave her a kiss that sent heat streaking to the darkest corners of her soul. "I've missed holding you, Lily. I've missed you touching me like this and me touching you. It's all I've been able to think about for three weeks. But you've had a lot of trauma in the past several days and I won't take advantage of that. I came in here to comfort you and I promise that's all that's going to happen."

As she stared up at him, she realized that he was trying to do what he felt was honorable. But was that what she wanted? To simply be held by the man she loved? Possibly for the last time?

Considering his views on love and having children, they had no future together. She knew that and, although it made her sad, she had accepted the inevitable. Could she resist one last night of knowing the strength of his lovemaking and the ecstasy of their bodies coming together as one heart, one soul?

"You wouldn't be taking advantage of the situation," she said, realizing that her decision had already been made. "I want you to make me forget that outside the doors of this house there's a world waiting to intrude." She kissed his strong jaw. "I want you to make love to me, Daniel."

She watched him tightly close his eyes and swallow hard before opening them again as he eased her to her back. "Are you sure that's what you want?" he asked, propping himself on one elbow to stare down at her. "I'd rather go take a dozen cold showers than to have you regret one minute of my making love to you."

"There are a lot of things I'm not certain of," she said honestly. "But I do know that no matter what tomorrow brings, I won't regret being with you tonight."

It was apparently all the assurance he needed to hear, because, without hesitation, Daniel lowered his head to capture her lips with his. Teasing and coaxing, he masterfully built her anticipation of deepening the kiss and when he did take it to the next level, his tongue stroking hers sent a tingling wave of excitement flowing throughout her entire body.

As he explored her inner recesses, he moved his

hand down her side to the tail of her nightshirt. His fingertips grazing her thigh as he slowly inched the garment upward caused a shiver of pure delight to race up her spine and she had to remind herself to breathe. But when he continued up her side to the swell of her breast, then paused to worry her taut nipple with the pad of his thumb, heated sensations spread to every cell in her being.

Unable to lie still, Lily raised her shoulders to help him remove the nightshirt. She wanted to feel his hands over every part of her and she wanted to touch all of him as well. In one smooth motion, he tossed her night-shirt over the side of the bed, and the feel of her sensi-tive skin pressed to his bare flesh caused the stirrings of an empty ache deep in her core.

Running her hands over his chest and abdomen, she reacquainted herself with the width of his shoulders and the dormant power lying just beneath his smooth skin. She loved his body, loved that it contrasted so perfectly with her softer feminine form.

"I'm going to love every inch of you," he murmured against her skin as he nibbled his way down to her col-larbone and beyond. "And when I get done, there won't be a doubt left in your mind how much I've wanted and missed you these past few weeks."

The promise in his voice caused a quiver of anticipa-tion to course through her. When he reached the slope of her breast, then kissed his way to the sensitive tip, her breath caught and a coil of need began to tighten deep inside her. She held his head to her when he took her into his warm mouth. Unable to stop a tiny moan of pure pleasure from escaping, she reveled in the many sensations he was creating inside her. He was driving her completely insane and she loved every minute of it.

"Does that feel good, Lily?" he asked as he trailed his lips down her abdomen to her stomach.

"Y-yes."

He traced the elastic waistband of her panties with his finger. "Do you want me to stop?"

"I-if you do…I'll never forgive you," she said, gasping for breath.

His deep chuckle seemed to vibrate all the way to her soul. "Sweetheart, there's no way I could stop now." When he slid his hand down inside her panties, she automatically raised her hips to help him and in no time, the scrap of silk and lace joined her nightshirt on the floor. "Those three weeks without you have felt like a lifetime."

Before she could tell him that she felt that way too, he caressed her side, her hip and the inner part of her thigh. Her heart pounded against her ribs as she waited for his touch. When he finally cupped the soft curls at her apex, then slipped his fingers inside to stroke her with tender care, the aching desire he created was almost more than she could bear.

"P-please…Daniel," she gasped, reaching down to find him. She gave to him as he was giving to her, but she wanted more. She wanted him to fill the empty ache that threatened to consume her. "I…need you now."

Lily felt him shift as he removed his underwear, then the feel of his body pressed to hers, his arousal strong against her thigh, caused an answering flutter in her lower belly. She wanted him to join their bodies, to make them one heart, one mind, one soul.

"Sweetheart, I got so carried away, I forgot that I

don't have anything to protect you," he said, his voice filled with regret.

"There's, um, no need…to worry about that," she assured him.

"It's a safe time of the month?" he asked as his fingers continued to excite her in ways that she could have never imagined.

"Mmm."

She knew she was being evasive and that it was unfair not to tell him that there was no need to protect them from what had already happened. But she wanted this one last time with him, wanted to store up the memory for the empty nights that lay ahead of her.

With no hesitation, he parted her legs with his knee, then levered himself over her. Reaching down, she guided him to her and Lily closed her eyes as she savored the exquisite feelings of becoming one with the man she loved.

"Open your eyes, sweetheart," he commanded when their bodies were fused completely. "I want to watch your pleasure build until you can't wait any longer. Then I want to watch you the moment I take you over the edge."

Gazing into his eyes as he slowly began to move within her, she felt as if she might drown in the dark blue depths. Heat spiraled throughout her being and ribbons of excitement threaded their way to the ever-tightening coil deep within her as her body responded to his rhythmic thrusts. Holding on to his broad shoulders to keep from being lost, Lily felt her feminine muscles begin to contract around him as Daniel fulfilled his promise of creating a passion in her so strong that she lost sight of where he ended and she began.

Time seemed to stand still as the tension inside her built to a crescendo, then suddenly broke free to send waves of pleasure coursing all the way to her soul. Moments later, Daniel groaned and she felt him stiffen inside her as he found his own shuddering release. When he buried his head in her shoulder and collapsed on top of her, Lily held him close as they both slowly drifted back to reality.

Loving the feel of him still inside her and the weight of his large body covering hers, when his breathing eased and Daniel moved to her side, she felt a deep sense of loss.

"Are you all right?" he asked, pulling her close.

She wanted to tell him that she loved him—would always love him—but it wasn't what he wanted to hear. Instead, she nodded. "That was perfect."

"Oh, I still have a few tricks up my sleeve that will make it even better the next time," he said, kissing the top of her head.

"You're not wearing a shirt," she teased. "How could you possibly have anything up sleeves that don't exist?"

"Hush, woman," he said, laughing. "Rest assured, I have more ammunition in my sensual arsenal that I'm going to take great pleasure in showing you."

She knew that once he learned about the baby, that would change. But snuggling against him, she decided to face that in the light of day, along with all the other recent harsh realities of her life.

The first light of day had just started to peek through a part in the bedroom drapes when Daniel lay his arm over Lily's stomach to draw her close. He smiled at the feel of her soft curves nestled at his side. Last night had been mind-blowing and he still couldn't get over how much he had missed Lily's uninhibited response to his lovemaking. She was so receptive to his touch, and the fact that she wasn't the least bit shy about touching him in return never failed to arouse him in ways a man could only dream of.

He propped himself up on his elbow to stare down at her sleeping so peacefully beside him. He had even missed waking up in the mornings with her warm bare skin against his hair-roughened flesh. Not that they had spent the entire night together all that often, but he had forgotten how pleasant it was to wake up with her the few times that they had.

Watching her sleep, he frowned. He wasn't entirely sure he was comfortable with how easily he had gotten used to the little things like waking up next to Lily or how cute he found her propensity to crowd him on his side of the bed. It certainly wasn't something he missed about his ex-wife. Of course, Charisma would have had to sleep with him more than a few times a month for him to have become accustomed to having her next to him in bed.

Daniel lay back and pillowed his head on his folded arms. His ex-wife had used sex as a bargaining tool—a way to coerce him into buying her a new pair of diamond earrings or the little red Ferrari she just had to have for her trips to the mall. Otherwise, she slept in the master bedroom, while he was perfectly content to sleep in a room down the hall.

But that was one thing he never had to worry about again, he thought contentedly. He was single and intended to stay that way.

He glanced over at the sleeping woman beside him.

Whatever he and Lily had going on between them was special and, without outside interference from his mother, they would be together for as long as it lasted. Then, when the time came for them to stop seeing each other, he would go his way and she would go hers. No hard feelings and no emotional pain for either of them.

As he lay there patting himself on the back for keeping his life simple, Lily moaned and stirred next to him. He wondered if she was having another nightmare until she sat straight up in bed, threw back the covers and bolted for the bathroom.

"What the hell?" He grabbed his underwear from the pile of clothing on the floor and pulled them on, then knocked on the closed bathroom door. "Are you all right, sweetheart?"

When she failed to answer, he tried the knob. The door was locked.

"Lily, what's going on?" he demanded.

"P-please go…away," she said a moment before he heard the sounds of her being sick.

"As soon as you're able, open the door," he said, wondering what could have caused the upset.

Retrieving her pink fluffy robe from the closet, every possible reason that might have caused her to be sick ran through his mind as he waited outside the closed door. It couldn't be a case of food poisoning because they had both had the same thing for lunch and skipped dinner and he was fine. Of course, she might be sick because she hadn't eaten. Or maybe it was a delayed reaction to learning that her father had been murdered. That coupled with the media circus outside her mother's place and the fact that the police intended to question the family was enough to cause anyone's nerves to get the better of them.

When he finally heard the click of the lock being released, he was waiting for her when she opened the bathroom door and after helping her into her robe, walked her over to sit on the end of the bed. "I'll be right back," he said, going into the bathroom to wet a washcloth. Returning to the bedroom, he knelt in front of her and patted the cool, damp terry cloth over her cheeks and forehead. "Feeling better now?"

She nodded. "Daniel…" She paused to take a deep breath. "We have to talk."

"Why don't you lie down and rest a little more?" he suggested. "We can discuss whatever you like after you're feeling better."

"I have to tell you now," she said shaking her head. "Otherwise, I might lose my nerve."

Something in her tone caused the hairs on the back of his neck to stand straight up. "What?"

He watched her close her eyes, then she took another deep breath and looked him square in the eyes as she announced, "I'm pregnant."

"Pregnant."

A mixture of shock and disbelief coursed through him and it suddenly felt as if all the oxygen had been sucked out of the room. Slowly rising to his feet, he walked over to sit in the chair across the room. Propping his forearms on his knees, he stared down at his loosely clasped hands as he tried to wrap his mind around the single most life-changing word of his life.

"You're pregnant," he repeated, knowing he sounded like a damn parrot, but unable to stop himself.

It had been the last thing he expected her to say. Lily

was pregnant and there wasn't a doubt in his mind it was his baby.

"The baby is the reason I've been sick in the mornings but ravenous the rest of the day," she said, her tone a bit unsure. "It's also the reason I've been so tired and have to take naps in the afternoon."

Daniel opened and closed his mouth several times as he tried to decide what to ask first. Should he question her about when she discovered the pregnancy? Should he ask when the baby was due? Or should he find out how she wanted to handle things? How the hell was a man supposed to deal with something he thought he'd never face?

"How did this happen?" he finally asked when he found his voice. When she gave him a look that suggested she thought he might be a little simpleminded, he immediately shook his head. "Strike that. I know the biology. I'm just trying to figure out when it could have happened. We were always careful."

"I think it might have been the night after Thanksgiving." She sighed. "If you'll remember, we got so carried away we didn't think about protection until after the fact."

He nodded. "That was the only time it could have happened. But when did you find out about the pregnancy?"

"The morning of your mother's dinner party," she said, sounding a bit hesitant. "I was going to tell you that night after the party, but—"

"Charlotte had her little talk with you first."

"How did you know about that?" Lily shook her head. "I didn't say anything."

"You didn't have to," he said, getting up to pace

the floor. "After I thought about it, I realized that you had stopped taking my calls and refused to go anywhere with me right after the party. And knowing my mother's penchant for snide comments and sticking her nose where it doesn't belong, it all added up. Then, when I asked her about it, she admitted it." He stopped pacing as a thought occurred. "If we hadn't run into each other in the lawyer's office the day your father's will was read, would you have told me about the pregnancy?"

She stared down at her hands, but there was no hesitation when she nodded. "I was going to tell you right after the holidays, but with Daddy dying and all that has happened since, I could never seem to find the right time."

"Lily, we both know better than that," he said, shaking his head. "There were plenty of times in the past week that you could have told me."

When she looked at him directly, there was a defiance in her expression that he had never seen before. "You're right. I could have told you, but I wasn't sure your knowing was in my best interest until the pregnancy was a little further along."

It suddenly dawned on him what she meant. "You thought I would ask you to put an end to it, didn't you?"

"I wasn't sure," she said, shaking her head. "But I wasn't going to give you the chance to try to talk me out of having my baby."

Walking over to kneel in front of her, he took her hands in his. "Lily, you have to believe me. I wouldn't ask you to do anything like that. It's true that I never intended to have a child, but that doesn't mean I won't take responsibility for the baby if you choose to have it."

She suddenly straightened her shoulders as her expression changed to one of pure defiance, then rising to her feet, she picked her nightshirt off the floor. "That isn't necessary, Daniel. I'm perfectly capable of loving and raising my baby on my own without your help." She motioned for him to look around as she walked over to the dresser and removed some clothes. "As you can see, I have a huge house now with more than enough room for half a dozen children if I want them. And believe me, I won't think of a single one of them as a responsibility. Having a child is a blessing and one that I'm really looking forward to."

Before Daniel could react, she walked into the bathroom and slammed the door. The sound seemed to echo throughout the room and galvanized him into action. He needed to think, needed to decide how to handle this latest development.

Taking a quick shower, he dressed and went downstairs to see if they had brought coffee when they moved most of Lily's food the day before. As he waited for the coffeemaker to work its magic, he wandered out onto the terrace. The January sun shone brightly across the backyard and highlighted the quaint beauty of the paved courtyard. He saw none of it.

Lily was having his baby. Un-freaking-believable.

What he found even more incredible was that he wasn't nearly as upset with the idea of being a father as he had always thought he would be. Was he still in a state of shock? Or was he just mellowing with age?

Having never entertained the idea of fatherhood, he had really never given thought to how he would react if he did impregnate a woman. He was sure as hell giving it his undivided attention now.

What kind of father would he be? Given that he was an only child, raised by two people who had no business procreating, he really didn't have an example of what parenting was all about. Hell, since becoming an adult, he had never even been around kids, let alone a baby.

He ran his hand over the tension building at the back of his neck. It wasn't like getting a car. At least vehicles came with extensive instruction manuals and directions on where things were located and how to troubleshoot certain problems. The last he heard, the hospital might send a few pamphlets along when parents took a new baby home from the hospital, but otherwise they were on their own to figure things out.

And how were he and Lily going to manage custody of the child? Whether he had intended to be a daddy or not, he wanted to be a part of his kid's life and he didn't care much for the idea of having contact with him or her only a few days a week.

No, if he was going to be a father, he was going to do this right. And he knew just what that meant.

Taking a deep breath, he walked back into the kitchen and eyed the wine rack. He could use a drink and if it were a little later in the day, he would definitely pop the cork on a bottle of merlot. Instead, he would have to rely on a good strong cup of coffee to get him through what he had to do.

Twenty minutes later when Lily entered the kitchen, he sat at the table sipping his coffee and wondering how she was going to react when he told her about his decision. "Are you feeling better?"

"A little." She filled a teakettle with water, set it on

the countertop range, then opening one of the cabinets, reached for a box of crackers on the top shelf.

Daniel quickly left the table and got the box for her. "Is this all you're having for breakfast?" he asked, frowning. "Shouldn't you be eating something a little healthier?"

"Weak tea and crackers sometimes helps to settle the queasiness," she explained, taking a tea bag from one of the canisters on the counter.

"Why don't you sit down and let me make the tea for you?" He gave her what he hoped was an encouraging smile. "I can tell you still aren't feeling one hundred percent."

For a moment he thought she was going to refuse, but, shrugging, she put a few crackers on a small plate and walked over to sit at the table. "The nausea usually runs its course by midmorning," she said, nibbling on one of the crackers.

Once he had the tea made and took his seat across the table from her, he asked, "Are you up to discussing your announcement?"

She finished the cracker, then took a sip of tea before she answered. "I don't know that there's anything to talk about, Daniel. To me this baby is a precious gift. But all you see is an inconvenient obligation."

"Sweetheart, you have to understand," he said, reaching across the table to cover her hand with his. "Being a father is something that had never crossed my mind and it came as a shock that I'm actually going to have a child. I've never been around kids and I'm man enough to admit that I'm going to be treading in unfamiliar waters. But when I said I would take responsibility, what I meant was that I intend to do my best to man up and be a good parent."

"That's not the way it came across when you said it," she murmured, her expression dubious.

"I'm sorry for that," he said, meaning it. "But I give you my word that, even though we didn't plan on this happening, I'm going to do the right thing by you and the baby."

She stared at him a moment, before she vigorously shook her head. "No. Don't you dare—"

"You're going to be the mother of my baby," he interrupted her. "And as soon as the arrangements can be made, I'm going to make you my wife."

Six

"Oh no you're not," Lily said, pulling her hand from his. "Up until an hour ago, making me or any other woman your wife wasn't even a consideration for you. You can't sit there and tell me that your views on marriage have suddenly taken a hundred-and-eighty-degree turn just because I told you I'm pregnant."

"Sweetheart, I don't think you should be getting this upset." He sounded so calm, so self-assured, that she wanted to bop him across the top of the head with something. "I'm sure it's not good for you or the baby."

"You don't have the slightest idea of what is or isn't good for us," she stated flatly.

"I'm going to take care of that with a trip to the mall as soon as it opens," he said, apparently undaunted by her accusation. "I'll buy every book I can find on pregnancy and taking care of an infant. Rest assured, by the time you give birth, I'll know everything that's going on with you and the baby."

Unable to sit still, she rose from the table. "Daniel, I think it's admirable that you want to learn all you can about babies and that you want to be a good parent. But marriage isn't a requirement to do that."

"I realize that, Lily," he said, standing to face her. "But our getting married is what I want."

Placing her fingertips to her temples, she massaged the tension that was building into a pounding headache. "No, Daniel, getting married is not what you want and if you weren't so stubborn, you would admit it."

"A baby needs both its parents together," he insisted. "And you and I already have a lot going for us."

She barely kept her mouth from dropping open. "Like what? Making love?"

The rat had the audacity to grin. "Well, there's that. You can't deny that we both enjoy what we have together in bed."

"There's a whole lot more to a marriage than pleasing each other sexually." How on earth could he think it was that simple?

"It's a good start," he said, reaching out to take her into his arms.

"You're actually serious, aren't you?" She couldn't believe they were having this conversation. "What about trust and mutual respect?"

"If you didn't trust me, you would have never gone to bed with me, Lily," he said reasonably. "And it's out of respect that I'm asking you to marry me."

"Oh, yeah, that's what every woman wants to hear," she said, not even trying to keep the sarcasm from her voice. Pulling from his arms, she put distance between them as she held up her hand to tick off the reasons she was refusing his offer. "Number one, I won't marry you because you didn't ask. You *told* me that was what we were going to do."

"Would you prefer I get down on one knee?" he asked, smiling.

She ignored his glib question. If she didn't, she might do him bodily harm. "Number two, I wasn't born yesterday. Knowing your views on the subject, I'm not fool enough to believe that you had a miraculous turnaround when you heard the word *pregnant*." She held up another finger. "Number three, and for me, the most important reason of all that I refuse to marry you, is that you don't love me."

"I don't believe that love is a requirement for marriage," he said, straightening his shoulders as if bracing himself for battle.

"And I believe it is," she said, knowing that they had reached an impasse. Suddenly feeling defeated, she shook her head. "I'm going upstairs to lie down before I call to see if the media has stopped camping out on my mother's front lawn. Please, lock the door and set the alarm when you leave."

"I'll get the truck on my way back from the bookstore," he called after her as she walked from the room. "We'll talk more this afternoon while we move the rest of your things. But make no mistake about it, Lily, we will be together."

Lily didn't bother telling him that there wasn't anything left to be said. She had taken a stand and she wasn't going to back down. Besides, he wasn't listening anyway.

Lying down on the bed, she hugged one of the pillows close to her chest in an effort to stop her heart from feeling as if it were breaking. She had known from the gossip at the many charity events she'd attended the past few years that Daniel Addison wasn't the type of man a woman pinned her hopes and dreams on. He didn't want a home, a loving wife and children. He was perfectly content leading the life of one of Charleston's most eligible bachelors. But when he introduced himself and asked her to dance that night at the Children's Hospital Autumn Charity Ball, the moment he took her into his arms, she had foolishly fallen in love with him.

Now he was telling her he wanted them to be married, but it wasn't for the right reasons. She wanted the fairy tale of love and happily-ever-after, while all he wanted was to do what he deemed to be socially acceptable.

Tears filled her eyes and ran down her cheeks. She didn't want a marriage like the one her mother had apparently had with her father, didn't want to wake up one day and find that Daniel had a second family in another town.

Turning to her side, she squeezed her eyes tightly shut against the thought. She didn't think Daniel had a long-lost love he was searching for, but then that had probably never crossed her mother's mind about her father, either.

The scent of Daniel's clean masculine body on the pillow caused her tears to fall faster. He'd held her, made love to her, and as much as she would like to pretend that he was the prince she would one day share the castle with, he wasn't.

Daniel didn't love her and probably never would. And she refused to settle for anything less from him.

When he unlocked the door to the Beauchamp mansion and reset the alarm, Daniel set the bag of books and the suitcase full of his clothes on the hall bench and headed straight for the master suite upstairs. He had waited to leave until he was sure Lily had fallen asleep and he was fairly certain she wouldn't awaken until he returned from his trip to the mall bookstore. He had intended to get one of the Addison Industries pickup trucks to move the rest of her things on the way back, but once he saw the headlines on the front page of the Charleston newspaper and a report from the morning news crew stationed on the Kincaids's lawn, he had decided against it.

The media seemed determined to get a comment from one of the family members about the latest development in Reginald Kincaid's death and confirmation on the rumor that he had been leading a double life for several decades before the homicide. Daniel was just as determined that Lily was not going to be the one they harassed. She had enough to deal with. Not only was she having to get used to the fact that someone had murdered her father, she was pregnant and having to adjust to the idea of becoming his wife. She didn't need the added stress of being pursued by a horde of reporters as they tried to scoop each other on the story.

When he entered the master suite and walked through the sitting room, the French doors opened to the bedroom beyond alerted him that Lily was already awake. "How are you feeling after your nap?" When she didn't answer, he checked the rest of the suite. She wasn't there. "Lily?" he called, hurrying out into the hall.

His voice was met with silence and he wasn't sure whether he should start looking for her on the floor above or take a chance that she was out in the carriage house. Deciding to search the entire house before he headed outside to see if she was in her studio, he climbed the stairs leading to the third floor.

"Lily, sweetheart, are you up here?"

Nothing.

He wasn't a man who was prone to worry, but he was becoming more concerned with each passing minute as he went from one bedroom to the next, looking for her. Her car was still at her mother's place, therefore it was unlikely that she had left on her own. He quickened his steps. He didn't even want to think about the fact that Reginald Kincaid's killer was on the loose with few clues as to who it was or if the person intended to target anyone else in the Kincaid family.

When he turned to start back down the stairs, he noticed that the door at the end of the hall, the one leading up to the cupola, was open. Taking the steps two at a time, he was relieved when he found her standing at the windows, staring out at Charleston Harbor.

"Isn't this breathtaking?" she said, pointing out at the view. "I can see the Sullivan's Island Lighthouse and Fort Sumter."

Daniel glanced out over White Point Gardens at the harbor beyond. The scenery was nice, but he liked the view inside the cupola a whole lot better.

Lily looked amazing. She had pulled her long red hair up into a ponytail with some kind of puffy, dark green fabric band, exposing the smooth, creamy skin of her slender neck. He barely resisted the urge to pull her close and kiss every inch of it. Instead, he concentrated on the bulky emerald sweater and snug jeans she was wearing. The sweater looked soft and the color complemented her hair and vivid blue eyes perfectly. But when she bent over to pick up her sketch pad and pencil from the floor, the denim pulling tight across her shapely backside caused the air to lodge in his lungs and sent his blood pressure soaring.

"Did you get the truck?" she asked, straightening to face him. "I haven't heard from RJ, but I'm sure the media must have cleared out by now."

"I don't think that's the case," Daniel said, shaking his head to clear it. "When I stopped by my place after going to the bookstore, I saw a live report from your mother's front lawn on the news. The press is still trying to get an interview with a member of your family and I don't think they're going anywhere until they do."

"Why are they being so persistent?" she asked, frowning. "We don't know any more about what happened to Daddy than what the police released in their statement yesterday evening."

"I'm not sure, sweetheart." He couldn't resist touching her smooth cheek as he tried to decide whether to tell her that the media had also gotten wind of Reginald's secret life up in Greenville. "When a man as successful as your father is found at his office desk with a bullet in his head, whether it was self-inflicted or a homicide, investigative reporters are going to try to dig up everything they can."

"Was there anything in the paper about Angela Sinclair and her two sons?" she asked hesitantly. He knew she was hoping that part of the story would stay under wraps for a bit longer.

Daniel reluctantly nodded. "Right now, it's being reported as a rumor they are trying to verify."

"But it won't take long before that happens," she said, her expression not at all happy. "I just wish everyone would leave us alone long enough to deal with Daddy's loss and the revelations about the Sinclairs."

He didn't hesitate to put his arm around her shoulders and pull her to his side. "I wish it could be that way, too."

She wasn't pulling away from him and he hoped she had come to the conclusion that their getting married was for the best. But he wasn't stupid enough to bring up the subject this soon. He would give her a little more time to realize that it was the perfect solution.

"So I'm going to have to hide out here for a while longer before I'm able to move the rest of my things?" she asked, oblivious to his speculation.

"I would say it will be the first part of the week before we're able to move what's left." He shrugged. "If you want to get out of the house for a while, we could always go back to the aquarium and feed the stingrays. You enjoyed that."

"Thank you for the offer, but I think I'd rather stay here and finish putting things away." She shook her head. "But don't think you have to stay with me. I found a small stepladder in the basement. If I need to put something on one of the top shelves, I can always use that."

"Like hell you will." He turned her to face him and, putting his hands on her shoulders, met her startled gaze. "You're not getting anywhere near that ladder. Is that clear?"

"Oh, really?" Her eyes narrowed. "What gives you the right to tell me what to do?"

"I'll be the first to admit that I know next to nothing about pregnant women, but do you really think that a fall would be good for you or the baby?" He knew if she thought about it she wouldn't take the chance of something happening that might jeopardize the pregnancy. But her heated response was an indication that she still wasn't happy with him.

"I hadn't thought of that," she admitted grudgingly. "But don't feel that you have to stay here with me. I'm sure you have other things you'd rather be doing."

He blew out a frustrated breath. "Lily, I'm not going anywhere now or in the future. While I was out, I stopped by the condo and picked up some of my clothes—"

She glared at him. "Don't you think that was rather presumptuous of you?"

"When I told you this morning that we're going to be together, I meant it," he said, unconcerned by her protests.

He wasn't about to upset her further by telling her that he wouldn't even consider leaving her alone at night until after her father's killer had been caught. For that matter, he wasn't all that happy about having to leave her alone during the day to go to his office, but there was no way around it. His only consolation was that during daylight hours, there would be too many witnesses in the park across the street.

"And I told you—"

"Hush," he said, pulling her to his chest as he lowered his mouth to hers.

At first Lily started to push away from him, but as he moved his lips over hers, he could feel her body relax until she dropped her sketch pad and sagged against him. Deepening the kiss, he marveled at her eager response and the sweet taste of her desire. She might still be upset with him, but she couldn't resist him any more than he could resist her.

The thought had him aroused in two seconds flat and if he didn't put a little distance between them, he wasn't entirely certain he could keep from making love to her right there in the cupola. Considering there was nowhere but the floor to do that, Daniel reluctantly broke the kiss.

When he lifted his head and took a step back to gaze down at her upturned face, he didn't think he had ever seen her look more beautiful. With her cheeks rosy from the blush of desire and her eyes bright with passion, it took every bit of willpower he had not to take her back into his arms.

Deciding that he needed a diversion, he bent to pick up the sketch pad at their feet. He eyed the drawing of the cupola's interior. "What's this?"

She blinked as if coming out of a trance before pointing to the sketch. "I thought that having a window seat around the entire perimeter in here would be a nice addition. I could sit up here and sketch or just watch the ships and boats in the harbor."

He glanced at the pad of paper, then looked around the area inside the cupola. "There should be just enough room if it's not too wide," he said, nodding. "When are you going to have it built?"

She shrugged as she started down the stairs to the floor below. "Probably not until spring."

An idea began to take shape as he followed her downstairs to the kitchen. It shouldn't take more than a day to get the project completed. If he could find a way to get her out of the house long enough, having it built would be a nice surprise for her and quite possibly get him back in her good graces.

"What do you have planned for the last Saturday of the month?" he asked, thinking of a contractor friend of his who owed him a favor.

"I have an exhibit of my illustrations at the mall bookstore for a couple of hours that afternoon," she said as she pulled the makings for sub sandwiches from the refrigerator. "Why?"

"I thought it might be fun to plan a day seeing some of the sights," he said, thinking quickly. "We could take one of the tour boats out to Fort Sumter in the morning and then visit the Charleston Museum in the afternoon."

"I haven't been to those places in a few years," she said thoughtfully. "It might be nice to visit before the tourist season starts."

"Why don't we plan the outing for a week from today then," he said. It was going to cost him extra for his friend to build the window seat on such short notice, but if it made Lily happy, then it would be well worth whatever he had to pay.

She stopped making sandwiches to meet his gaze. "Daniel, it's not going to work."

"What?"

"If you think moving in here and taking me places is going to get me to change my mind about marrying you, you're wrong." She shook her head. "I know what

I want and it's something you can't or won't give me. Either way, I'm not settling for anything less."

"Let's just go and have a good time," he suggested. "I give you my word that I won't pressure you to do anything you don't want to do."

As they ate lunch, Daniel thought about what Lily said. He knew she wanted him to love her, but how could he give her what he wasn't even sure existed? Love was something he hadn't experienced much of throughout his life and certainly not during his disastrous marriage.

He supposed his mother loved him as much as she was capable of loving, but when he was growing up, her idea of showing him how she felt had been to pat him on the head, hand him a hundred-dollar bill and send him off to the arcade. His father had been even worse at showing how he felt about his only son. The few times George Addison had tried to be affectionate, more times than not the gestures had been awkward and clearly embarrassed the hell out of the man. Of course, their cook Rosemary had always made it clear that she was extremely fond of him, but Daniel had never heard her verbalize that she actually loved him.

Staring across the table at Lily, he knew he cared for her. There was certainly no question that he desired her. But love?

"Daniel, are you listening to me?" she asked, interrupting his disturbing introspection.

"I'm sorry, I was thinking about something at the office," he lied. "What were you saying?"

"I asked if you would like to go to my brother's with me on Thursday evening to babysit my three-year-old nephew," she said, taking a sip from her glass of milk.

More comfortable with her question than with his own thoughts, he concentrated on answering her. "Do you think your brother would mind me tagging along?"

She shook her head. "I can't see why Matt would have any objections. Besides, this will give you a glimpse of what it's like to care for a child and how you relate to one."

He knew she expected him to decline the invitation and up until learning he was going to be a father, he probably would have. But he wanted her to see that he really was serious about being a good parent and it couldn't hurt to see what he should expect down the road when their child was a bit older.

Giving her an agreeable smile, he nodded. "Helping you babysit sounds like a great idea. I think I would like that. A lot."

As Lily watched Daniel get down on the floor to help Flynn build a skyscraper made of oversize Lego bricks, she couldn't help but marvel at how well he was doing with her nephew. From the moment they had walked into Matt's house, Flynn seemed to charm the socks off Daniel and she could tell Daniel was having a good time interacting with the little boy. For a man who had never spent time around a child, he seemed to be thoroughly enjoying the experience.

"It's almost time for bed," Lily said, checking her watch. "While I make your bedtime snack, why don't you show Daniel how well you put your toys away, Flynn."

Always well behaved, Flynn nodded and started putting the blocks into their plastic canister. "Dannel, help pick up the blocks, please," Flynn instructed, managing Daniel's name as best he could. Flynn's vocabulary was excellent for a child his age, but he still had a little trouble with some words.

When Lily stepped to the door to tell them the snack was ready, she smiled as she watched the exchange between her nephew and his new best friend.

"Here you go," Daniel said, picking up the last of the blocks, then getting up from the floor to stretch.

"Come on, Dannel," Flynn said, holding his hand up to take Daniel's. "Time for my snack."

As Lily watched, Flynn led Daniel past her into the kitchen. "I share," Flynn said when they were all seated. He picked up his spoon and dipped it into the small cup of pudding in front of him. "I a good sharer."

"Thank you, Flynn, but I'm not really hungry," Daniel said, ruffling her nephew's dark brown hair. "But I promise the next time I come over I'll have some pudding and milk with you. Will that be all right?"

With a spoonful of pudding in his mouth, Flynn nodded vigorously.

While her nephew ate his snack, Lily smiled at Daniel. "You looked as if you enjoyed yourself this evening."

Daniel glanced over at Flynn shoveling more pudding into his mouth. "This little guy makes it easy to have fun." He gave her a grin that made her feel warm all over. "Thank you for letting me help you babysit."

"You're very welcome," she said, smiling back as she wiped Flynn's hands and mouth. Picking up her nephew from his booster seat, she kissed his baby-soft cheek. "Are you ready to take your bath and get your pajamas on before I read your bedtime story?"

Throwing his arms around her neck, Flynn gave her

a hug. "Your book, Aunt Lily." When she set him on his feet, he walked over to where Daniel sat at the table, his expression serious. "You stay for the story."

"I'm going to be here as long as your Aunt Lily," Daniel reassured the child.

"C'mon, Aunt Lily," Flynn said, taking her hand to tug her along. "Dannel wants to hear the story."

"We'll only be a few minutes," Lily said, amazed that Flynn had taken to Daniel so quickly.

Ten minutes later, as they walked back into the family room with Flynn dressed in his pajamas and holding the book he had picked out, Lily watched as the little boy crawled up into Daniel's lap. "Do you want Daniel to read the story this evening?" she asked.

"No. You," Flynn answered, resting his head back against Daniel's shoulder.

With her nephew sitting on his lap and Daniel cradling the little boy with one arm, Lily was touched by the sight. What was there about a man being so attentive and gentle with a child that she found sexy?

Opening the book, she decided that her pregnancy hormones must be working overtime. She was finding everything about the way Daniel dealt with her nephew to be heartwarming and she looked forward to seeing him with their own child.

As she read the story, she kept glancing over at Flynn and watched as his eyes began to droop. When she was sure he had fallen asleep, she closed the book and started to get up.

"What happens next?" Daniel asked, grinning. "Did the puppy find his way back home?"

"Of course." She laughed softly. "Children's books always have happy endings. But why did you want to know how the story ends? You didn't get that caught up in it, did you?"

"I wanted to know what to tell him if he quizzes me the next time we babysit," Daniel answered as he got up from the chair and shifted her nephew to where Flynn's head rested against his shoulder. "If you'll lead the way, I'll carry him to bed for you."

He intended to accompany her the next time she had to babysit?

Lily shook her head as she walked down the hall ahead of him and her sleeping nephew. Daniel was apparently very serious about learning to deal with children so that he could be a good parent and she was glad. She wanted him to love their child, even if he couldn't love her.

When they tucked Flynn into his bed and walked back to the family room, Daniel sat down in the armchair while she seated herself on the couch. "So what do you think?" she asked. "Do you feel a little more relaxed about being around children?"

"Absolutely," he said, smiling. "I wasn't sure how the evening would go, but I really did have fun. Flynn is a great kid."

"I think so," Lily said, "but then I'm prejudiced because he's my nephew and I love him to pieces."

They fell silent a moment before Daniel asked, "Where's his mother?"

"Grace was killed in a plane crash about a year ago," Lily said sadly. "She was on her way for a weekend visit with her parents when the chartered plane went down, and my heart aches for both her and Flynn. She wanted him so desperately, but she was robbed of the opportunity to see him grow up. And although Matt is trying to keep her memory alive for him, Flynn won't know his mother except in pictures and on video."

"That's tragic," Daniel said, his tone filled with compassion. He frowned. "You made it sound as if it wasn't easy for them to have the little boy. Was there a problem with her getting pregnant?"

"I'm not exactly sure what was wrong, but Grace wasn't able to conceive and I'm not sure that she would have been able to continue the pregnancy if she had," Lily said, yawning as she curled up in the corner of the couch. "That's why they finally decided to go with in vitro fertilization and use a surrogate to carry a baby to term."

He rose from the chair and, walking around the coffee table, joined her on the couch to put his arm around her. "I'm sure it's been hard on your brother. Losing his wife and trying to juggle being a single father with all that's going on now at The Kincaid Group couldn't possibly be easy."

"It really has been difficult for him, and I'm worried about him." Her heart ached for Matt and all the tragedy that he had been through in the past year. "He was devastated when Grace was killed and now he's torn between being with Flynn and working practically day and night to get these reports ready for..." She paused as she tried to hide another yawn. "Jack Sinclair."

"Why don't you give up and take a little nap?" Daniel suggested.

"I can't go to sleep. I'm babysitting," she said, unable to resist laying her head on his shoulder.

"I'm awake." He kissed the top of her head. "If there's a problem I can't handle, I'll let you know, sweetheart."

"Well, I might close my eyes for just a few minutes," she said reluctantly.

She hated to shirk her duties as a babysitter, but Daniel was there to wake her in case Flynn needed her. And she was having such a hard time keeping her eyes open that maybe resting them for a bit would help.

Daniel smiled. He knew as soon as Lily closed her eyes that she had fallen asleep. From everything he'd been reading in the books he had bought at the mall, it was quite common for a woman to need extra rest in the first few months of her pregnancy, then again the last month or so before she gave birth.

Gazing down at the woman who was going to have his baby, he couldn't believe how drastically his views had changed in such a short amount of time. If someone had told him just a week ago that he would be embracing the idea of becoming a father and doing his best to convince a woman to marry him, he would have laughed his head off. But now?

After spending time with Lily's nephew and finding that he wasn't a complete washout with kids, Daniel found that he was actually looking forward to the day when he could sit on the floor and do things like build a Lego skyscraper with his own son or daughter. It was something his own father had never even attempted when Daniel was a boy and he couldn't help feeling they had both come out losers because of it. His father had missed the opportunity of knowing the wonder of the world as seen through the eyes of a child and Daniel had missed out on having a real dad, not just a man who only made a halfhearted attempt to relate to him.

Placing his hand on Lily's still-flat stomach, he

thought about what an amazing mother she was going to be, too. As he watched her with Flynn throughout the evening, he had marveled at how kind and patient she was—suggesting that he pick up his toys instead of ordering him to do it and allowing him to make choices of the book he wanted to read and who he wanted to read it. And she wasn't the least bit uncomfortable showing the toddler plenty of affection.

Several times in the past few days, he had wondered what kind of parents they were going to be. But not anymore. They were going to make a great team, raising this child. And that led him to a more immediate problem. How was he going to convince Lily to marry him?

He had been true to his word when he told her that he wouldn't pressure her into doing anything she didn't want to do when he started staying with her at the mansion. But he was finding that he wasn't a patient man when the stakes were this high. He wanted their baby to have a set of parents who not only worked together to raise him or her, he wanted their child to have a mother and father who bore the same last name.

He had made up his mind and, although it hadn't been an easy decision, come to terms with the fact that he was again going to wade into the pool of matrimony. Now all he had to do was find a subtle way to convince Lily to get her feet wet with him.

And as far as he was concerned, the sooner that happened, the better.

Seven

"Who on earth could that be?" Lily muttered as she hurried down the hall. No one but her family and Daniel knew she lived here and he had left over an hour ago to go to his office.

Crossing the foyer, she hoped it wasn't someone from the newspaper or television stations. The reporters had been relentless trying to get an interview and forced her mother to make the decision to cancel the family's Sunday dinner last week, as well as the coming week's get-together. A day or two after the news broke that her father had been murdered, Laurel had released a statement that the family didn't know anything more than the police and asked that they please respect the Kincaids's privacy as they mourned the death of their loved one. Instead of quieting things down, the press release only seemed to fuel the media frenzy.

Looking through the peephole in the center of the door, she half expected to see a member of the press standing on the piazza. What she didn't expect was to see Charlotte Addison standing on the other side.

Lily was almost tempted to pretend she wasn't home or that she hadn't heard the doorbell. Her father had warned her that she would have to deal with Daniel's mother at some point and putting it off wasn't going to make it any easier. She took a deep breath and steeled herself for an unpleasant confrontation.

"Hello, Mrs. Addison," she said, opening the door.

The woman looked taken aback. "What are you doing here?" she asked, raising one disapproving eyebrow.

"I moved in a week ago," Lily answered, noticing there wasn't a car in the driveway or one parked along the street in front of the house. Had the woman walked the half mile from her home on East Battery?

"I saw lights on last night when I returned from a meeting of the planning committee for this year's Read and Write charity event, but I just assumed someone had rented…" She shook her head. "It's not important. What does your mother intend to do with this place?"

Lily would have liked to tell the woman that it was none of her business. But she couldn't ignore the years of Southern etiquette her mother had taught her from the time Lily was old enough to listen—always show elders respect and courtesy even in the face of other people's rude behavior.

"My mother doesn't own the mansion, Mrs. Addison," Lily said, trying her best to keep her irritation in check. "I do. My father left it to me in his will."

To Lily's surprise, Charlotte Addison smiled. "Then

we shouldn't have any problem coming to an agreement."

Lily had no idea what the woman was talking about. "Excuse me?"

"This is my ancestral home and I want it back," the woman said as if Lily's father had stolen it from her.

"It's not for sale, Mrs. Addison," she said firmly. She might have allowed the woman to bully her into doing what she wanted once, when Charlotte wanted Lily to stop seeing Daniel, but Lily wasn't going to let it happen a second time. "I've loved and admired this house all my life and it was my father's wish that I have it."

Charlotte's expression darkened. "How could you possibly care so much for a piece of property that you have no ties to?"

"But I do." Lily pointed to White Point Gardens across the street. "When I was a little girl, my father used to take me for walks in the park and I would spend hours sitting on that bench across the way, staring at this house and dreaming of living here."

"A child's fancy," the woman scoffed, but her complexion had turned a bit pale and Lily noticed that she looked as if she wasn't feeling well.

"Are you all right, Mrs. Addison?" she asked, growing concerned.

"I...think I need to sit down for a moment," Charlotte said, sounding a bit shaky. She kept staring at Lily as if transfixed.

"Please, come in and I'll get you something to drink," Lily said, taking the woman's arm to help support her.

No matter how Charlotte Addison had talked to her

in the past, she was Daniel's mother and the grandmother of the baby Lily was carrying. Besides the fact
that she had been brought up to lend her assistance to
someone when there was a need, Lily really didn't want
to see anything bad happen to her.

Once Lily had Charlotte comfortably seated on the
couch in the formal sitting room just off the foyer, she
hurried to get the woman a glass of water. When she
returned, Mrs. Addison looked as if she might be feeling a lot better.

"Do you need to put your feet up, Mrs. Addison?"
Lily asked, handing her the glass. "Should I call Daniel?"

"No," the woman said a little too quickly. There
was a hint of panic in the one word and Lily sensed
that Mrs. Addison didn't want Daniel knowing she had
paid Lily a visit. "My blood sugar or my blood pressure might be a bit low," Charlotte said, taking a sip of
water. "I'll be fine. Really."

Having had a childhood friend with juvenile diabe-
tes, Lily knew that if it was low blood glucose, Charlotte needed to eat something. "I was just making a
turkey sandwich for myself. Why don't you come into
the kitchen and I'll make one for you as well."

For the first time since Lily had met her, Mrs. Addison looked a bit unsure. "I don't…want to impose."

"Nonsense," Lily said, helping her to her feet. "It's
no trouble at all." As she escorted Charlotte down the
hall, she wondered how on earth she managed to get
herself into situations like the one she was currently in.
But she couldn't in good conscience send the woman
on her way without making sure she was going to be
all right.

While Lily made sandwiches for them, she noticed that Mrs. Addison, although silent, kept looking around at the renovations that had been made to the mansion. "Do you like the restoration my father commissioned?" she asked, setting the food in front of Charlotte.

"Yes, it looks…surprisingly nice," the woman said begrudgingly.

"If you're up to taking a tour after we eat, I'll show you the rest of the house," Lily offered.

She wasn't certain why it should matter to her, but she wanted Charlotte to see that the man she had more or less accused of stealing the home from her had cared enough about the place to see that the once-elegant antebellum mansion had been restored to its original grandeur. Lily fully expected her to refuse, considering Charlotte's bitterness toward Lily's father, but she felt compelled to try to vindicate him in the woman's eyes, if only a little.

"Yes," Mrs. Addison said, surprising her. "I think I would like that very much."

When Daniel walked through the rear entrance of the Beauchamp house, he thought he might be hallucinating. Seated at the table in the kitchen with Lily was his contemptuous, opinionated mother. What the hell was she up to this time?

"Hello, Daniel," Charlotte said, surprising him with her almost congenial tone.

"Charlotte," he said, giving her a slow nod of acknowledgment. What was going on?

Glancing at Lily, he tried to judge her mood. His mother had a knack for rubbing people the wrong way with little or no effort. Knowing how Charlotte felt about Lily and her family, he fully expected that she had dialed up her condescension several notches once she learned a Kincaid was living in Beauchamp House. But Lily didn't seem the least bit upset. In fact, just the opposite. She appeared to be quite relaxed and at ease with his mother.

"Lily, could I see you in the foyer for a moment?" Turning his attention to Charlotte, he added, "We'll only be a few minutes."

When Lily followed him down the hall to the entryway and well out of earshot of Charlotte, he asked, "Why is she here?"

"It's all right, Daniel," Lily assured him. "Your mother stopped by on her morning walk to inquire about the house and I invited her to come in when she seemed to become lightheaded."

"Is she all right?" He had never known Charlotte to be sick a day in her life, but she was a little over sixty and could be developing problems.

"She's fine now," Lily said, assuring him. "I asked her if she would like to have lunch. After we ate, I showed her the renovations that Daddy had made."

"She hasn't been giving you attitude over your dad or our seeing each other?" he asked, unable to believe that was all there was to his mother's visit.

"Not really." She shook her head. "She did tell me that she wanted to buy the mansion back, but I told her it wasn't for sale."

"And Charlotte accepted that?" he asked.

"Not at first." Lily shrugged. "I told her that I loved this place and about how long I've dreamed of living here. After she saw how much time and effort went into the renovations, I think she realized I was serious about my feelings for it and accepted that I won't be selling it." She glanced down the hall toward the kitchen. "We really should get back to her. It's rude to leave someone alone like this."

Daniel shook his head to clear it as he and Lily returned to the kitchen where his mother sat gazing out of the floor-to-ceiling windows at the courtyard beyond. What could have caused Charlotte's turnaround? And why?

He didn't believe for a minute that she had shown up on Lily's doorstep to inquire if the place was for sale, then gave up that easily. Nor was he buying her sudden change of heart about the Kincaids. Charlotte didn't operate that way.

After sitting at the table listening to Lily and his mother exchange polite conversation while he ate lunch, he wasn't entirely certain he hadn't somehow landed in the twilight zone. Charlotte was being quite civil and he knew his mother well enough to know that her tone was completely sincere. She was actually enjoying herself. Unreal!

When he finished eating, he checked his watch. "I hate to eat and run, but I have a meeting in about an hour and I need to get back to the office," he said, rising to his feet. He picked up his suit jacket from the back of the chair and put it on. "I'll be going past your place if you'd like a ride home, Charlotte."

"Yes, I think I'll take you up on that offer," she said as she stood up. Turning to Lily, she smiled. "Thank you for lunch. It's been nice chatting with you. You and Daniel will have to come over sometime for dinner."

"That would be nice," Lily said, smiling

The exchange between the two women in his life

was almost more than he could comprehend and Daniel couldn't wait to get Charlotte into his car. A change in attitude that drastic had to have been brought about by something and he wanted to know what it was.

Escorting his mother to the car, he quickly slid in behind the steering wheel. "What was that all about, Charlotte?"

To his mother's credit, she didn't try to act as if she didn't know what he meant. "She really does love Beauchamp House, doesn't she?"

"Yes, she does," Daniel answered as he drove the car out onto the street. "Living in Colonel Sam's old place has been a dream of Lily's her entire life."

"If not entirely happy about it, I can be content with her owning the property as long as I know she cares that much about it," Charlotte said decisively.

"Who are you and what have you done with my mother?" he asked, meaning it. "I would have thought a Kincaid living there would have sent you into orbit."

"I'll admit that at first I was livid to learn that Reginald's daughter had inherited the property, but she is Elizabeth Winthrop's daughter, too, and that counts for something," Charlotte explained. "The Winthrops have been in Charleston as long as the Beauchamps, and until Elizabeth married that scoundrel, their background was impeccable. Now that Kincaid is gone, I suppose her error in judgment can be overlooked."

"And that's all it takes to make Lily living there okay with you?" he asked, unable to get over his mother's screwed-up reasoning. "Kincaid is dead and that restores Elizabeth's standing in the social pecking order?"

Charlotte shrugged. "That and the fact that the girl

is pregnant with a Beauchamp descendant who will be residing in the mansion with her."

Shocked that his mother knew about Lily's pregnancy, Daniel steered the car over to the curb, to turn and stare at his mother. "Lily told you about the baby?"

"Oh, no," she said, shaking her head. "Lily didn't say a word. She didn't have to."

"Then how—"

"Have you ever heard of the 'pregnancy glow'?" Charlotte interrupted.

He shook his head. It sounded like something made up. "No, I can't say that I have."

"It's more pronounced with some women than it is with others," Charlotte went on quite seriously. "It has something to do with the hormonal changes and a woman's complexion. Lily definitely has it."

Now Daniel knew he had entered another realm. Never in a million years would he have believed he would ever be listening to Charlotte explain the changes caused by pregnancy.

"When may I expect my first grandchild?" Charlotte asked.

"Mid or late August," he heard himself tell her. The whole conversation was so surreal, Daniel wasn't entirely certain he wasn't dreaming.

"And when are you going to make an honest woman of Lily?" his mother asked as calmly as if they were discussing the weather.

"That's hard to say," he answered, steering the car back into traffic. "You did a lot of damage with your meddling before Christmas and she isn't overly receptive to the idea just yet. But I'm working on it."

"Is there anything I can do to help things along?" Charlotte asked, shocking him yet again.

"Good God, no." The last thing he needed was his mother's interference.

"This could be my only grandchild, Daniel," Charlotte said sternly. "I don't want him or her to be born on the wrong side of the blanket, nor do I want us to be strangers."

"You really mean that, don't you?" he asked.

Charlotte nodded. "I thought that after you and Charisma divorced, my chances for becoming a grandmother had died along with your marriage." She turned in the bucket seat to face him. "No matter what you believe about me, most of which is probably true, I do care and want to be part of your child's life."

"I'm glad to hear that, Charlotte, but this is between me and Lily. Whether we get married is our decision. I want you to stay out of it. I do, however, give you my word that you will get to know the child." Parking the car outside Charlotte's home, he got out and opened the door for her. "It's not common knowledge that Lily's pregnant and I'd rather you not say anything to anyone about it until we're ready to announce the news ourselves."

"I won't." She raised one eyebrow. "Does Elizabeth know?"

"Not that I'm aware of." Walking her up the front steps to the wide porch, he noticed that his mother wore a smug expression. He almost groaned. "What's going on in that devious head of yours this time, Charlotte?"

"It appears that I'm the first of the grandmothers to

know about the baby," she said, sounding somewhat triumphant.

Shaking his head, Daniel walked back to his car. Some things never changed. He should have known that Charlotte would somehow find a way to feel superior to Elizabeth Kincaid.

At the moment, his mother's head games were the least of his worries. He had to make a trip to the contractor's office to drop off a key to the Beauchamp house for the builders to add a window seat to the cupola, then he had to get to his meeting with Lily's sister.

Kara Kincaid had built a solid reputation as an event-planning genius and he was in desperate need of her help. If she could assist him in setting up and initiating something to convince Lily to accept his proposal of marriage and become his wife, he would forever be grateful to her. And he was finding that getting Lily to say yes was becoming more important to him with each passing day.

"Have you seen this, Daniel?" Lily asked as they walked through the natural history exhibit at the museum. "I wasn't aware that we had so many prehistoric animals in Charleston."

"Yeah, about twenty-eight million years ago," he answered, laughing. "Haven't you ever been through this part of the museum before?"

She shook her head. "When I was little, all these mounted skeletons gave me nightmares."

"Boys must be a lot different about these kinds of things than girls," he said thoughtfully. "The dinosaur bones were always my favorite part of coming to the museum when I was young. I even thought I wanted to be a paleontologist when I grew up."

"My favorite exhibits are the ones with the dresses and jewelry." She couldn't help but smile. "I love seeing how women used to dress. Can you imagine how grand it must have been with all those beautiful gowns twirling around the dance floor at a ball and all the jewels sparkling in the glow of the candlelight?"

"No. Not really."

She smiled at the frown on his handsome face. "No, I don't suppose boys care much about hoopskirts and necklaces made of precious gems."

"Are you sure you don't have time to write children's books?" he asked, grinning. "You certainly have the imagination for making up stories any little girl would love to read." He took her hand in his and brought it to his lips. "If our baby's a girl, I'll let you take the lead on teaching her about dresses and jewelry. I'll take care of coaching her softball team."

"And if the baby's a boy?" she asked.

His grin made her feel warm all over. "We won't make you suffer through looking at the bones of an eighteen-foot-long crocodile or the primitive toothed whale skeleton."

"Thank you. You have yourself a deal." She couldn't help but shudder at how horrible the animals had to have been when they were roaming the area. "I think I can safely say I won't be changing my mind about that, either."

Strolling through the museum with Daniel, Lily couldn't help but think about how wonderful it had been since he moved into the mansion with her. He had kept his word and hadn't put any pressure on her to invite him back into the master suite or agree to marry him, giving them time to learn even more about each other. She would have never dreamed that he liked classic movies or that he wasn't a big fan of sailing.

But their time together had also taken a toll—at least on her. Loving him the way she did, it had been extremely difficult to have him kiss her goodnight, then watch him walk down the hall to one of the guest bedrooms, while she entered the master suite alone.

She sighed. How much longer could she go on being so close to him without having him touch her? Love her?

As they continued on through the museum, she realized they had wandered into the room displaying examples of historic weaponry of the past three hundred years. "This is another area where you can take the lead," she said as a chill ran the length of her spine. "If you don't mind I think I'll skip this and meet you later by the entrance."

"Don't like swords and muskets, huh?"

"Not particularly."

His expression suddenly became remorseful and he immediately took her by the elbow to guide her out of the room. "Lily, I'm sorry. I should have realized this exhibit would drag up painful emotions."

"I suppose antique guns won't always remind me that my father was killed with one," she said, glad to be away from the weaponry area. "But right now, it's just a bit too soon."

Moving from one glass case to another in the textile section, Lily forced herself to forget about the guns and concentrate on the elaborate ball gowns. She couldn't help but wonder if their baby would be a girl or a boy. It really didn't matter to her which gender the baby was just as long as he or she was healthy. Although, it would be fun to share the beauty of the historic dresses with her daughter.

"Do you want a boy?" she asked as they strolled toward the exit of the museum.

Daniel shrugged. "I think every man would like to have a son." When they stepped out into the fading sunlight of late afternoon, he took her into his arms. "But I would be just as happy with a little red-haired girl with her mother's blue eyes."

"Perfect answer, Mr. Addison. You're going to be a wonderful father."

Lily couldn't resist raising up on tiptoe and kissing him soundly.

As she stared into his navy blue eyes, she knew she had lost the battle she had waged with herself for the past week. She wanted Daniel, had never stopped wanting him and she knew in her heart that would never change.

She nibbled on her lower lip a moment before she whispered, "I've missed having you hold me."

The heat in his gaze indicated that he knew exactly what she meant. "I've missed making love to you, too. But why did you have to tell me that now?" he asked, groaning as he rested his forehead against hers. "Now I'm going to rush you through dinner so that we can get back to the mansion."

"Why?" She knew, but she couldn't resist teasing him. "I thought you made reservations at that new five-star restaurant you've been wanting to try."

Nodding, he put his arm around her waist and pulled her to his side as they walked toward his car. "No matter how good the food is, I'm not going to know whether I'm having beef bourguignon or filet of boot leather."

"Really?" She laughed. "What makes you think that?"

He opened the car door for her to get in, then leaning inside, gave her a kiss that curled her toes. "Because all I'll be able to think about is taking you in my arms and loving you all night long."

Throughout dinner, Daniel seized every opportunity to touch her hand, give her meaningful glances and tell her how much he wanted her. By the time they walked out of the elegant French restaurant, Lily wasn't sure which one of them was more eager to get home—him or her.

Several minutes later when they arrived at her house, instead of taking her right upstairs to the master suite as she anticipated, Daniel took her hand in his and led her to the flight of stairs going up to the third floor.

"Where on earth are we going?" she asked, following him.

"You'll see," he said, opening the door to the steps leading up to the cupola. When they reached the top, he instructed, "Now close your eyes. I have something I want to show you."

She had no idea what he was up to, but she could tell he was impatient for her to see whatever it was. Closing her eyes, she heard him flip on the light switch a moment before he led her up the last step to the cupola.

"Open your eyes, Lily."

When she did, she caught her breath at the sight

of the beautiful window seat encircling the perimeter of the tiny room. "Oh, Daniel, I love them," she said, touching the aqua print fabric of the plush cushions. "This is exactly what I envisioned." Turning to put her arms around his neck, she gave him a quick kiss. "Was this the reason you insisted we stay out the entire day?"

"I had to make sure the contractor had plenty of time to get them finished," he said.

With his arms around her waist, holding her close against his solid frame, she felt as if she could stay that way forever. "I love everything about them and I love... that you thought to do this for me."

Gazing into his blue eyes, she watched them darken to navy as he gave her a smile that stole her breath. "I'm glad you like them, sweetheart."

She had wanted to tell him she loved him, but sadly, it wasn't what he wanted to hear. "Please kiss me, Daniel."

"Sweetheart, I thought you'd never ask," he said a moment before he took a step back to turn off the lights to ensure privacy.

When he returned to her, his mouth settled over hers and Lily gave herself up to the mastery of his kiss. Daniel might not love her, might never feel the emotion that filled every cell of her being, but that didn't stop her from loving him.

She knew she was playing with fire and there was a very real possibility that she would end up getting burned. But she couldn't seem to stop herself. No matter how much she wanted to protect herself from the emotional pain she might suffer, he was, and probably always would be, her biggest weakness.

As he deepened the kiss, she abandoned all thought

and reveled in his exploration. Compelled to do a little exploring of her own, she engaged him in a game of advance and retreat, tracing his lips, then slipping past them to stroke his tongue as he had done hers. His answering groan sent heat streaking throughout her entire being. She wanted him to know how she felt, needed him to feel the strength and power without her saying the words. She belonged to him as she would belong to no other man and she intended for him to know that.

When he slid his hand down along her side, then tugged the tail of her silk blouse from the waistband of her skirt, Lily anticipated the touch of his hands on her sensitized skin. Helping him to free the garment, she reached for his belt buckle.

"Just a minute, sweetheart," he said, breaking the kiss.

He put just enough distance between them to unbuckle the strap of leather at his waist, then pulled his shirt from the band of his trousers. Taking her back into his arms, he slipped his hand beneath her blouse and skimmed it along her ribs to the swell of her breast. When he covered her with his warm palm, her heart skipped several beats and she felt as if her knees were going to give way.

She suddenly felt herself being lifted off her feet and she realized when he placed her on his lap that he had settled them both on the new window seat. The feel of his strong arousal pressed to the side of her hip and the touch of his hand as he gently caressed her breast caused her head to spin, and the need growing within her became almost unbearable. She wanted him—needed him. Now.

"Hey, where are you…going?" he asked when she pulled from his arms to stand up.

She glanced at the windows of the cupola and the night sky outside that was so dark she could barely see her hand in front of her face. Reassured that they were concealed from prying eyes, she smiled as she knelt in front of him to release the closure at the top of his waistband, then reached for the tab at his fly.

"Lily…are you sure about…this?" He sounded as if he had run a marathon.

She nodded as she slowly ran her fingernail down the zipper and the bulge beneath straining to be freed. There were a lot of things that she was unsure of, but loving him wasn't one of them. If she couldn't tell him how she felt, she intended to show him.

"You are about to get so-o-o lucky, Mr. Addison."

Daniel held his breath as tooth by tooth, Lily eased the zipper down, releasing him from the confines of his pants. One of the many reasons he had been attracted to her had been her free spirit, her spontaneity. But never in his wildest dreams would he have imagined the circumstances in which he found himself at that moment. Every man had his share of fantasies, but all his paled in comparison to the reality of what was happening to him now.

When Lily had the zipper completely lowered, he felt as if his head might fly right off his shoulders when she used her index finger to trace him through the cotton of his boxer briefs. He had never experienced anything more erotic in his entire life as from base to tip, she painstakingly measured his length and girth. By the time she reached the elastic at his waist and he raised his hips to help her pull his underwear down his thighs, Daniel decided if he died at that very moment, he would leave the world a very happy man.

When he reached for her, Lily surprised him when she shook her head. "Not yet, darling."

He was smoldering hot and it appeared she was getting ready to add more fuel to the flames. "Sweetheart, I think I'd better…warn you. You're playing… with fire," he said through clenched teeth.

The touch of her hand on his heated body caused his heart to race, but the first touch of her lips kissing him intimately drove his blood pressure into stroke range. Daniel squeezed his eyes shut and tried to concentrate on maintaining his control, but it was damn difficult with Lily slowly driving him to the brink of insanity.

Unable to remain passive any longer, he reached down to lift her to her feet. "Let's go downstairs to the master suite."

She surprised him when she shook her head. "I need you now."

When she slipped her hands beneath her skirt to remove her panties, then straddled his hips, he thought he might die of ecstasy as her body slowly consumed his. "Don't…move," he warned.

"Why?" Her warm breath feathering over his ear almost sent him into total meltdown.

"Because if you don't remain completely still, there's a very real possibility this could be the shortest lucky streak on record," he said, knowing it was going to take every ounce of his stamina to keep that from happening.

When he felt he had regained enough control to ensure her pleasure, he kissed her, then placing his hands on her hips, urged her into a rocking motion against him. Heat suffused every fiber of his being and he knew he had never experienced with any other woman the degree of passion, the deep insatiable hunger, that he did with Lily. She made him feel whole for the first time in his life.

Deciding not to delve into what that might mean, Daniel concentrated on Lily's body tightening around him and he knew she was close to reaching the pinnacle. Just when he thought he might lose the battle he had been waging with himself, he heard her soft moan at the same time her body intimately caressed his.

Daniel groaned deeply as her pleasure unleashed the tide that had been building inside him. Holding her tightly against him, he wasn't sure he could keep from passing out as the intensity of his release sent waves of pleasure surging through him.

Never before had making love been as powerful, as all-encompassing. He felt in his heart it never would with any other woman. Only Lily.

And that's when he knew. He had finally found the emotion that had escaped him all his adult life—the feeling that he hadn't even been sure existed.

He had fallen hopelessly in love with Lily Kincaid.

Eight

On Monday, Lily nervously sat in police headquarters in downtown Charleston, waiting to be interviewed about her father's homicide. "Please state your name, age and your relationship to the deceased, Miss Kincaid."

"I'm Lily Kincaid, I'm twenty-five and the youngest daughter of Reginald Kincaid," she said, surprised that her voice sounded so steady, considering the state of her jangled nerves.

"Where were you on the evening of December thirtieth, the night your father was murdered?" Detective McDonough asked.

As the lead detective on her father's murder investigation, Charles McDonough had explained in advance that her statement would be recorded and that his questions would be straightforward and to the point. He had told her that he wanted her answers to be just as concise.

But she hadn't expected him to be so blunt. Hearing the word *murder* to describe her father's death was almost more than she could bear. At times she still found it difficult to believe her father was gone, let alone that someone had taken his life.

A chill ran the length of her entire body as she reflected on how her father had to have known his killer and had most likely let whoever it was into the office building that night. The security at TKG was too tight for him not to have let the person inside. Either that or the murderer had access to the alarm system codes and knew the security guard's scheduled rounds. Either way, it left her with a horrible sense of dread. Could she know the killer?

"I was at the bookstore in the Shops at Charleston Place mall," she answered, pulling herself out of her disturbing speculation.

"What time were you there?" Detective McDonough asked.

"I arrived at the mall around six that evening and didn't leave until the store closed at nine." She remembered exactly when she had left because she and the bookstore manager had walked out to their cars together.

"Is there anyone who can corroborate your story?" McDonough asked.

"Yes, the manager of the bookstore, Mona Peterson, and several of her employees were present," she answered. How could it possibly be that the homicide detective managed to make her feel as if she were keeping something from him when she had absolutely nothing to hide?

Detective McDonough nodded. "What was the nature of your business at the bookstore?"

She had no idea what that had to do with catching her father's killer, but she supposed it was standard procedure for him to ask. "I'm an illustrator of children's books and I was helping to arrange an exhibit of my work to be displayed until this Saturday, when the author of the book will join me for a book signing."

She had considered canceling the appearance, but as Daniel had pointed out, her father's life was the one that had ended. Her life had to go on.

"Do you know of an acquaintance, either personal or professional, who might have threatened your father or have a motive for killing him?" the man asked, his expression stoic.

"No." She shook her head. "My father never discussed business with me and I really don't know of anyone who would want to do him harm."

"What about your family?" McDonough persisted. "Were there any strained relationships or estrangements?"

"No."

The man paused a moment. "What about his mistress and her two sons from up in Greenville?"

Lily hadn't expected the detective's questions to be easy, but she hadn't been prepared for him to ask her about her father's secret life. "I really don't know anything about them," she answered honestly. "The first I learned that they even existed was when they showed up at my father's funeral."

Detective McDonough stared at her for several long moments as if trying to judge if she was telling the truth. "Well, I think that's about it," he said, closing a file on top of the table in front of her. He gave her a pointed look. "We will be checking out your story to see if you were where you indicated. If you have any changes you wish to make to your statement, now would be the time to do it."

Relieved that the interrogation was finally over, Lily shook her head. "No. To the best of my knowledge, everything I've told you is correct."

"Thank you for coming in to make your statement, Miss Kincaid." When she rose to leave, he opened the door to the small room where the interview had taken place. "If I have any more questions, I'll be in touch." Seemingly as an afterthought, he added, "If you think of anything that might help us with the investigation, please don't hesitate to give me a call."

As Lily left the police station and drove back to the Beauchamp house, she couldn't help but be relieved that her part in the investigation was over. The detective had told her that he would be interviewing everyone in her family separately and it appeared that he had started with her first.

She really didn't have anything to contribute to the investigation, but at least Detective McDonough knew she had an airtight alibi and could eliminate her as a possible suspect. Maybe once they whittled down the list of people who might have had contact with her father in his final hours, they would then be able to zero in on the horrible person who had committed the crime.

Steering her car into the driveway of the mansion,

Lily was surprised to see Charlotte Addison sitting on the piazza in one of the white wicker chairs by the front door, apparently waiting for her to return home. "Hello, Mrs. Addison," she said, getting out of her car. "I wasn't aware you were dropping by today. I hope you haven't been waiting long."

"No, I've only been here a few minutes," the woman said, surprising Lily with an actual smile.

Lily had no idea what caused Charlotte Addison's change of attitude toward her, but whatever it was, it had happened the day she stopped by to see if Lily was going to sell the mansion. But she wasn't going to question the about-face. Mrs. Addison was the mother of the man Lily loved and anything was better than the hostility the woman had displayed at the dinner party she'd hosted the week before Christmas.

"Would you like to come in?" Lily asked, not knowing what else to say when Charlotte fell silent.

"Well, maybe for just a few minutes." When Lily unlocked the door and stepped back, Mrs. Addison entered the house ahead of her. "I do have something I need to discuss with you."

"Would you like some tea?" Lily asked as they walked into the formal sitting room just off the foyer.

"No, thank you." Charlotte sat down on the edge of the couch, then directly met Lily's questioning gaze. "I know that in the past I may have been a little…shall we say, hasty with my opinion of you and your family," she said as if choosing her words carefully. "But I think that's behind us now and I feel we should forget about it and move on."

It appeared that Charlotte's acknowledgment that there had been a problem was as close to an apology as she was going to get. Lily really hadn't expected even that much from the woman.

"I think that would be best," Lily agreed. She thought they had moved past the issue when the woman dropped by the house while she was out walking the week before. Apparently Charlotte felt compelled to reiterate that she'd had a change of heart.

"The reason for my coming by today is to ask a favor of you," Charlotte said, finally getting to the point of her visit. "I think I mentioned the other day when I was here that I'm on the planning committee for the Read and Write charity event?"

"Yes, I remember you mentioning it."

The woman patted her perfectly coiffed hair as if putting it back into place. "Our maxim is 'promoting literacy in everyone from five to ninety-five,' and this year we've decided to hold a bachelor auction to raise funds for our programs." She frowned. "I wasn't altogether pleased with the idea of auctioning off men in order to raise money for such a worthy cause, but every bit of the proceeds will go to Read and Write, so I suppose it will be all right." She shook her head. "But I didn't stop by to tell you how undignified I think our means of raising money is this year. I wanted to ask if you would be willing to assist us."

"I think a bachelor auction will be all right, Mrs. Addison. It sounds like an excellent way to raise money." Lily approved of any cause to help further literacy and bachelor auctions were always popular. "What can I do to help out?"

"If possible, we need the use of this house." Charlotte's smile brightened as she explained further. "We often like to set some of our more elegant events in historic homes and since the renovations, the Colonel Samuel Beauchamp House would be perfect. The balcony just off the sitting room in the master suite here would be a lovely place for our bachelors to be spotlighted when they walk out for the bidding. They would be easily seen by everyone and the paved courtyard and large backyard could accommodate all our guests."

Lily nodded. Her privacy would only be invaded for one night and it was for a cause close to her heart. "I don't have a problem with that at all, Mrs. Addison. Is there anything else I can do to help out?"

"Excellent. And no need to worry, I think that we have everything else under control," Charlotte said, rising to her feet. "We'll have a tent set up with refreshments, so we won't need the use of the kitchen." As she walked across the foyer to the door, she turned back. "By the way, how are you feeling?"

"I'm doing just fine," Lily answered, wondering what could have caused the woman's concern. "Why do you ask?"

"Oh, no reason." Charlotte gave Lily a smile as if they shared a secret. "It's just that the other day you looked...a bit peaked."

The woman's knowing expression caused Lily to wonder if Daniel had told his mother about the baby. Could that be the reason Charlotte seemed concerned about her health?

"I'm doing fine. Really." Until she talked to Daniel and found out for sure, she wasn't about to discuss her pregnancy with his mother. Instead, she asked, "How are you doing? Any more problems with feeling lightheaded?"

The woman looked puzzled for a moment before she

shook her head, dismissing it as if it wasn't an issue. "I couldn't be healthier."

"That's good to hear, Mrs. Addison."

"Please, call me Charlotte," she said, shocking Lily even more when she gave Lily's arm an affectionate pat. "After all, you are…" She paused as if trying to find the right way to phrase what she wanted to say. "With my son now."

As the woman walked across the piazza and down the steps, Lily stared. Charlotte Addison was unreal. It had barely been a month ago that she had told Lily how unsuitable she was for Daniel. Now she was practically putting her stamp of approval on their being together?

There had to be a reason behind the woman's sudden change and when Daniel got home from the office, Lily intended to find out what it might be. She hadn't asked him not to tell anyone about the pregnancy, but she had assumed he would let her decide who they told and when they shared the news. And it wouldn't be long before she had to make that decision.

She nibbled on her lower lip as she closed the door and headed toward the kitchen for a snack before her nap. Her entire family was going to be at the bookstore on Saturday to show her their support, and because some of the more persistent reporters were still dropping by her mother's from time to time, they had decided to stop by the mansion after the signing for a family get-together. With all of them gathered, it would be the perfect opportunity to make her announcement about the baby.

Placing her hand on her stomach, she smiled. "You've got a big family who is going to be thrilled to hear that you're on the way." She almost laughed as another thought occurred. "And it appears you have a paternal grandmother who is pretty happy about you, too. Either that or she suffers from multiple personalities."

Seated in the reception area of The Kincaid Group offices, Daniel flipped through a magazine, then losing interest, tossed it on the coffee table in front of him as he waited for his meeting with RJ and Matt Kincaid. He was on a mission and as soon as he talked to Lily's brothers, his plans for this Saturday should come together nicely.

His meeting with her sister last week had been postponed at the last minute and he was glad that it had. At the time, he really hadn't had any ideas of what he wanted to do to convince Lily they should be married and hoped Kara would be able to think of something. But after acknowledging to himself how he felt about Lily, he knew exactly what he wanted to do and once he contacted Kara with the details, she had assured him that she would make it happen.

"Mr. Addison, RJ and Matt Kincaid will see you now," the secretary advised him.

Rising to his feet, he walked into the executive office to face Lily's brothers. "Thank you for seeing me on such short notice," he said, shaking both men's hands.

The brothers remained silent and Daniel could tell they were suspicious of him. He couldn't say he blamed them. Addison Industries was their chief rival and it probably felt as if the enemy had entered their camp. They had no idea he was paying them a visit for an entirely different reason than business.

"I suppose you're wondering why I wanted to meet

with both of you," he said, settling himself into a chair in front of RJ's wide desk.

"It did cross our minds," RJ said dryly as he sat down on the other side. The oldest of the Kincaid siblings, RJ was closest to his age and since Daniel's divorce, they had met up several times on the social scene. If there was a bigger player than Daniel had been before he met Lily, he would put his money on it being RJ.

"What can we do for you today, Addison?" Matt asked, standing just to the side of his older brother.

Both men's ties had been loosened and the buttons at the top of their collars had been unfastened. They looked overworked and extremely tired. Daniel could only guess how much pressure they had been under since the reading of their father's will.

Respecting the fact that RJ and Matt's time was at a premium due to the fact they were having to dance to Jack Sinclair's tune these days, Daniel got right to the point. "You both know I've been seeing your sister for the past several months and that I've been staying with her at the Beauchamp House. Since your father is gone, I thought I would talk to you and find out if either of you have a problem with me asking Lily to be my wife."

He could tell by the look on both their faces that he had taken the Kincaid brothers by surprise. But as Lily's sister Kara had pointed out, the plan they had come up with to convince Lily to marry him had a better chance of working if the entire Kincaid clan was on board with it.

A slow smile began to turn up the corners of Matt's mouth. "I don't have a problem with it and I know Flynn won't." He shook his head. "You're all my son has talked about since you and Lily babysat the other night."

"He's a great kid," Daniel said sincerely. "You should be very proud."

"I am," Matt agreed, beaming.

"As long as you're what Lily wants and she's happy, I don't have any objections," RJ said, grinning. "But I think I'd better warn you, Addison. Give her one minute of grief and you and I will have a come-to-Jesus meeting you won't soon forget."

"I wouldn't expect anything less from you, Kincaid," Daniel said, knowing how much Lily meant to her older siblings.

Outlining what he and Kara had planned and asking the brothers to participate, Daniel rose to leave. "I'll see you on Saturday."

"Good luck," both men called after him as Daniel left the office.

He purposely hadn't told any of Lily's siblings about her being pregnant. That would be up to her when and how she wanted to break the news to her family. Besides, he didn't want her thinking that he was trying to use the baby as leverage to get her family to convince her to marry him. She needed to know the reason he wanted to marry her was because he loved her, not because she was pregnant with his child.

As he drove from The Kincaid Group offices to the mansion, he went over his plan again. He hoped that he wasn't about to make a fool of himself in front of her family, as well as many of the good citizens of Charleston. Finding a way to tell her he loved her and getting her to believe him, then laying his heart on the line and asking her to marry him, came at no small risk to his pride, as well as his heart.

He had rejected the idea of love for so long that he knew Lily wouldn't believe him unless he could think of something that would convince her beyond a shadow of a doubt that he was sincere and ready to make the commitment of a lifetime. That's why he was pulling out all the stops to give her the rest of her dream.

Feeling pleased with himself for thinking up the idea, when he walked into the mansion ten minutes later, he stopped dead in his tracks. Lily stood on a chair in the middle of the foyer dressed in a long white dress with gold-and-purple trim, while her sister Kara knelt in front of her using pins to adjust the hem of the gown. Lily looked just like a princess.

"What's going on?" he asked, not happy with the whole damn scenario.

First off, he didn't like that his pregnant girlfriend was standing on a chair that could tip over with one wrong step. And second, he couldn't help but wonder if Kara or one of her other siblings had slipped up and told Lily about his elaborate plan. The whole idea hinged on surprise and he hoped it hadn't been ruined.

Lily smiled. "The bookstore manager called to ask if the author and I would mind dressing like characters from the book for the signing on Saturday." She laughed. "Since he wouldn't look right in a princess costume, I got the job. Fortunately, when I called Kara to see where I could get a dress on such short notice, she had one in her shop."

Relieved that she was none the wiser to the scheme, he couldn't help but grin. "So is the author going as a frog?"

"That's what I asked," Kara said around the pins she held between her lips.

"Since there isn't a frog in the book, that's doubtful," Lily said, turning for her sister to finish pinning the hem. "I think he's probably going to be dressed as the wise old wizard or maybe one of the ducks."

Daniel walked over to make sure Lily didn't fall from the chair. "If I were him, I'd opt for the wizard," he said, taking her hand to make sure she was steady. "It's a little more dignified than a duck." He had never been the type to hover over someone, but where Lily was concerned, he was finding it more difficult to resist with each passing day.

"Well, I think that does it," Kara said, sitting back on her heels. She started putting the rest of the pins back into a little plastic box. "As soon as you change, I'll take the gown with me and drop it off with the seamstress for her to hem. Then I think you should be all set for Saturday."

Lifting Lily down from the chair, Daniel waited until he was sure she had gone upstairs to the master suite to change before he asked Kara, "Is this dress-up thing for the bookstore real?"

"Well, it is now," she said, rising to her feet. Her green eyes twinkled mischievously as she confided, "I called and explained everything to the manager. She was more than happy to request that Lily and the author dress in character."

"Brilliant idea. Thanks." He could well understand now why Kara had built a solid reputation for being the best event planner in Charleston. Her ideas were extremely creative and her eye for detail was amazing.

"Oh, I almost forgot to tell you," she said, putting

the box of pins in her purse. "I did as you requested and told our mother all about your plan. She's going to be there, too."

"Excellent." When he heard Lily coming back down the stairs, he seized the opportunity to change the subject before she asked what they had been discussing. "How's your mother doing?"

"Surprisingly well." Kara shook her head. "Don't get me wrong, I'm proud of how well she's handled losing our dad, but I worry that she might not be dealing with all that's happened."

"I know what you mean," Lily said, handing her sister the gown. "I don't know about you, but to me, she didn't seem all that surprised when Angela Sinclair and her two sons showed up at the funeral."

Kara shook her head. "It's not just you, Lily. Laurel and I noticed that, too." She checked her watch. "Sorry to cut this short, but I'd better get going. I have just enough time to get this to the seamstress before she closes for the day. Then I have an anniversary dinner to oversee on Sullivan's Island this evening."

"Thank you for helping with my costume," Lily said, hugging her sister.

Kara hugged her back. "You know I'm happy to help. I'll see you on Saturday afternoon at the bookstore."

Daniel watched the exchange between the two sisters with interest. Being an only child he had often wondered what it would have been like to have a sibling— someone he shared a childhood history with. Watching Lily with her family, he couldn't help but think that life might not have been quite as lonely in the Addison household if he'd had a brother or sister.

"Your mother dropped by again today," Lily said when she closed the door behind Kara.

He groaned. "What was the nature of her visit this time?"

"It was actually quite pleasant." Lily told him about the charity event for literacy and his mother's request to use the house, then giving him an odd look, added, "Have you told your mother about the baby?"

"I didn't have to. Charlotte told me," he said, shaking his head. "Why? Did she say something?"

"Not really. She just kept smiling and asking how I feel." Lily frowned. "But how would she know—"

"When I took her home the other day, Charlotte told me that you have 'the glow.'" He put his arms around Lily to draw her to him. "I didn't believe her until I looked it up on the internet and sure enough, there it was." He shrugged. "It has something to do with hormonal changes causing a woman's complexion to look as if it's glowing. Apparently Charlotte knew what it looked like."

"I thought that was an old wives' tale." She looked a bit worried. "Do you think your mother has told anyone? I'd rather my family hear about the baby from me than to learn about it through the rumor mill."

"I asked her not to say anything," he assured Lily. "Charlotte might be intractable and at times downright obnoxious, but she's always respected my privacy when I've asked her to."

"That's good to know," she said, melting against him.

He loved the feel of her curvaceous body against his. Hell, he was finding that once he acknowledged the emotion's existence, he loved everything about Lily.

But if he told her now, he knew she wouldn't believe him. She would no doubt think he was just telling her what she wanted to hear to get her to agree to marry him. Even though that was exactly what he wanted her to do, he needed her to believe that he was sincere about his feelings for her, as well. He just hoped that what he had planned for Saturday was enough to convince her.

Later that night, after making love with Daniel, Lily snuggled close within the circle of his strong arms. "Did I tell you that my entire family will be coming to the bookstore this weekend, then stopping here for coffee and dessert afterward?"

"No, I don't remember you mentioning it," he said, sounding sleepy.

"Since Momma's had to cancel our family dinners the past two Sundays because of a few overly zealous reporters, she suggested the get-together." Lily pressed her lips to his shoulder. "I thought it might be a good time to let them all know about the baby."

He was silent for a moment and she thought he might have fallen asleep, when he finally said, "I'm sorry I won't be here when you tell them."

"You won't?"

He shook his head. "I won't be able to make it to the bookstore, either. I have an out-of-town meeting that I need to attend."

"How long will you be away?" she asked. A cold dread began to fill her chest.

"I probably…" he paused to yawn "…won't be back until sometime Monday."

She had never known Daniel to schedule a meeting

out of town or for that matter on a weekend. "Is this something that just came up?"

He nodded. "I met up with an old college friend I hadn't seen in years and we're going to spend the time catching up."

Pulling from his arms, Lily sat up and threw back the covers.

"Hey, where are you going?" he asked when she got out of bed to put on her robe.

"I...um, I'm hungry," she lied. When he started to get up with her, she shook her head. "You have to go into the office tomorrow morning. Go ahead and get your rest."

"Are you sure?" he asked, yawning.

Tying the sash on her robe, she nodded. "I'll be fine."

As she descended the stairs, Lily's heart thumped against her ribs and a sinking feeling settled in the pit of her stomach. Daniel's reasons for not attending the event at the bookstore and for skipping her family gathering sounded too much like the excuse her father had always used for his frequent trips out of town.

Tears filled her eyes. He knew how important the exhibit and signing at the bookstore were for her career and that she wanted him to be there with her. Why couldn't he have postponed the meeting with his friend until next weekend?

She had no reason to believe that what Daniel told her was anything more than what he said it was. To her knowledge, he had never lied to her, never led her to believe that he was anything but trustworthy. But how could she know for sure? Her mother had believed her father for three decades, only to learn of his betrayal when his mistress showed up at the funeral with her two sons.

Was she overreacting to the situation? Had learning about the double life her father had led for all those years affected her more than she realized?

Sitting down at the kitchen table, Lily stared down at her tightly clasped hands. She needed advice and she knew just the person to help her sort through her fears.

When she glanced at the clock on the microwave oven, she realized it was too late to call tonight. But when Daniel left for the office tomorrow morning, Lily was going to visit the woman she had turned to all her life when she needed guidance. She was going to talk to her mother.

Nine

"Momma, could we talk for a few minutes?" Lily asked when she found her mother sitting in the den reading a book.

"Of course, Lily." Her mother's smile and welcoming hug were already making Lily feel a little better. "What's bothering you, darling? You look as if you're carrying the weight of the world on your shoulders."

Lily wasn't surprised her mother knew something was wrong. Elizabeth Kincaid always knew when her children were upset and in need of her comfort and advice.

Sitting on the couch beside her mother, Lily couldn't seem to find a way to ask her mother what she wanted to know without it sounding as if she was prying. "Momma, did you ever suspect that Daddy had a secret life?" she finally asked.

Her mother remained quiet for a moment, then closing her book, took Lily's hands in hers. "Lily, I think deep down I've always known that your father's heart wasn't entirely mine. But I do believe he cared for me. And I know he loved all you children so very much." She gave Lily's hand a gentle squeeze. "Why do you ask?"

"I'm in love with Daniel Addison," Lily said, not knowing where else to start.

"I know, darling." Elizabeth smiled warmly. "Call it a mother's intuition if you like, but I've known for some time that Daniel is the one for you."

Lily shook her head. "I wish I could be as confident of that as you are."

"What makes you think differently?" her mother asked gently.

"He thinks we should get married, but he doesn't love me," Lily said, biting her lower lip to keep it from trembling.

"Oh, I'm sure you're wrong, darling," Elizabeth said, putting her arm around Lily's shoulders.

Deciding to tell her mother everything, she confided, "I'm pregnant."

"That's wonderful," Elizabeth said, hugging Lily close. "I'm thrilled that I'm going to be a grandmother again."

Lily knew her mother would be happy to hear about the baby. Family was everything to Elizabeth. "I thought Daniel and I could tell everyone after the bookstore event, but he's not going to be there with me. He has other plans."

Elizabeth lovingly kissed her cheek. "Where's he going to be?"

"He said he's going out of town to meet a college friend and..." Tears filled Lily's eyes. "It just sounds so much like what Daddy told you—told all of us—for all those years."

Her mother slowly shook her head. "Lily, you can't make Daniel pay for the mistakes your father made. It isn't fair to either one of you."

Was that what she was doing? Lily wondered. Had she suddenly started doubting Daniel simply because of what her father had done to her mother?

"The baby was the only reason Daniel told me he thought we should get married." Lily shook her head. "And he hasn't even mentioned that in the past couple of weeks."

"Daniel Addison has never impressed me as being a man who changed his mind so easily." Her mother nodded. "I'm sure he still wants to marry you. Maybe he's just giving you the space you need to decide that's what you want, too."

"I do want that." Unable to sit still, Lily rose to her feet and walked over to stare out the window at her mother's garden. "But is it asking too much for me to want him to love me?"

"I'm sure you're wrong about him not loving you." Her mother smiled. "I noticed the way he looked at you that first night when he asked you to dance at the Autumn Charity Ball for the Children's Hospital. I know in my heart it was love at first sight for him, Lily."

She feared her mother was wrong. "I wish I could believe that, Momma. But I don't think so. He doesn't believe in love and I won't settle for anything less from him."

"That's what he might think, darling," Elizabeth said, smiling. She left the couch to join Lily at the window. "Trust me on this. A mother knows these things. Daniel loves you with all his heart."

"But—"

"Give him time." Her mother gave her a comforting hug. "You'll see that I'm right."

On Saturday afternoon, Lily smiled until her face hurt as child after child insisted on having their picture taken with the Princess of Ducks. Not even the author of the book they were promoting, dressed as the wise old wizard, got as many requests. "Are you ready to leave?" Kara asked when the last child in line walked back to his mother.

"More than ready." Lily massaged her face with her fingertips. "I think I have a cramp in my cheeks from smiling so much."

"You make a beautiful princess," Elizabeth said, joining her daughters.

"Thank you, Momma," Lily said, hugging her mother. "But I think you're just a bit prejudiced."

"Aunt Lily a princess," Flynn said proudly as he and Matt walked over to them.

Bending down, Lily kissed her nephew. "Are you ready to go back to my house for ice cream and cake?"

"I don't know about Flynn, but I sure am," Matt said, grinning. "RJ and I worked through lunch so we could take off early to be here and I'm starving."

"Are you about finished gathering the information Jack Sinclair wants?" Lily asked, concerned. Both of her brothers looked tired and she knew they were under a tremendous amount of stress as they got the reports ready. Yet they had made the time to be there for her, while Daniel seemed to seize an excuse not to.

"We just have a few more things left," Matt said. "Then we'll have to wait and see what Sinclair has to say."

"Let's not discuss business today," Elizabeth suggested. "This is a day to celebrate Lily's accomplishments and success."

Lily could understand her mother's reluctance to listen to the details of yet another betrayal by their father. The fact that he had given the majority of TKG to his illegitimate son, while dividing up the rest between her children had to hurt their mother deeply, probably more than any of them realized.

"Lily, are you riding back to your place with Kara?" Laurel asked as she and RJ joined the rest of the family.

Lily nodded. "Kara brought me." Laughing, she added, "And unless she intends to make me walk home, she's stuck taking me back."

She still couldn't understand why her sister had been so persistent about driving her to the bookstore. But the moment Kara learned that Daniel wasn't going to be attending the event, she had insisted that she come by to get Lily.

As she and her family left the bookstore, Lily noticed that her mother and siblings all drove away from the parking area, while Kara seemed preoccupied with sending a text message on her cell phone. "Someone wanting you to plan their party?" Lily asked.

"Business is good," Kara said evasively as she smiled and started the car.

When they drove from the parking area, Lily couldn't help but feel sad. As much as she loved having her family at the event, the one person she wanted most of all to be there with her wasn't. Daniel had left early that morning for his trip and she didn't anticipate seeing him again for a couple of days.

"You're awfully quiet," Kara said as she drove them toward the Beauchamp house. "Is something wrong?"

"I was just thinking about how nice it was to have everyone there today." She did appreciate her family being there for her, but it was overshadowed by Daniel's absence.

"It would have been nicer if Daniel had been there, right?" Kara guessed.

"Yes." Apparently she hadn't been able to hide her disappointment as well as she thought.

When Kara parked the car in her driveway, Lily looked around. "Where is the rest of the family? They left before we did."

Shrugging, Kara followed her into the house. "Maybe they stopped to pick up something for our little get-together."

"Everyone drove separately," Lily said, shaking her head. "Why would all of them stop?"

"I don't know. Maybe they took a different route and they're held up in traffic." Kara motioned toward the stairs. "I didn't get a chance to see the house when I was here the other day. Why don't you give me the grand tour while we're waiting on them?"

"Sure. Just let me change and I'll show you around," Lily said as they climbed the stairs.

Her sister shook her head. "I'd rather you didn't take the dress off just yet. I'd like to get a picture of the entire family gathered around you still in costume."

Lily frowned. "Why?"

"For my scrapbook." Kara gave Lily a beseeching look. "Please?"

"Oh, all right," Lily said, giving in. She wasn't aware her sister had the time for scrapbooking. "We're already upstairs. Where would you like to start with the tour?"

"Why don't we start with the cupola and then work our way down?" Kara suggested. "I'd like to see the new window seat."

"How did you know about those?" She hadn't told anyone about Daniel having them built for her.

Kara looked a little startled. "I... Uh, Daniel mentioned them the other day. While you were changing out of the dress for me to take to the seamstress." Her cell phone chirped, indicating that she had another text message. When she checked the message, she smiled. "Lead the way. I'm dying to see the view."

"Don't you need to answer that?" Lily asked as they climbed the steps to the cupola.

"No, it was just a client letting me know his event is running on schedule," she said, pocketing the phone.

"If you have an event going on, why aren't you there?" Normally Kara was present at the parties she planned to see that things went off without a hitch.

"The view here is absolutely gorgeous," Kara said, instead of answering Lily. "You can see all the boats in the harbor."

Lily nodded as she gazed out at the big oceangoing ships and a few sailboats. "I'm assuming there will be more of the smaller boats in the spring and summer when it's warmer."

"Oh, look," Kara said, pointing toward the harbor. "Does that boat have something written on the main-sail?"

Looking in the direction her sister pointed, Lily squinted her eyes to try to focus on the boat sailing across the harbor. "How can you see that far away? Did you get new glasses?"

"Here." Her sister wore a knowing grin as she handed Lily a pair of binoculars she had removed from her purse. "Use these."

Lily frowned. "When did you start carrying binoculars?"

"Will you stop asking questions and just look?" Kara asked, grinning.

A bubble of hope began to rise in Lily's chest and her hands began to tremble as she took the binoculars from Kara. She had seen that look on her sister's face too many times not to know something was up. Looking through the lenses, she searched for the boat Kara mentioned and when she found it, her heart began to race and her knees began to tremble.

Daniel, dressed in a black tuxedo, stood on the deck. The message written in bold block letters on the pristine white mainsail read: I LOVE YOU, PRINCESS LILY.

Dropping the binoculars on the window-seat cushion, tears filled her eyes and she couldn't seem to stop shaking. "Daniel...loves me?"

Kara put her arm around Lily's shoulder. "Yes, he does."

"He doesn't like sailing," Lily said, picking up the binoculars for another look.

"He apparently loves you more than he hates being on a boat." She took the binoculars from Lily and ushered her toward the stairs. "Now, let's get down to the marina to welcome your prince when the boat arrives."

Her heart was so full of emotion it felt as if it might burst from her chest as Kara drove her the short distance to the marina. "When did the two of you… I mean, how did you manage…"

"Daniel got in touch with me almost a week ago," Kara said as she parked her car at the marina. "He knew exactly what he wanted and left it up to me to make it happen."

"I had no idea." Lily couldn't believe they had managed to arrange such an elaborate stunt in such a short time or that she had been none the wiser to the scheme. "Are you the one who arranged for me to be a princess today at the bookstore?"

"Guilty," Kara said, laughing. "I filled the manager in on everything. She and the author both thought it sounded like a lot of fun and after the success of the signing today, I wouldn't be surprised if more children's authors and illustrators are asked to dress in character."

As she and Kara hurried toward one of the slips where the sailboat would dock, tears streamed down Lily's cheeks at the sight of her family, Charlotte Addison and a crowd of curious boat owners lining the pier. At the end of the planked walkway, an arch made of gold, white and purple balloons marked the spot where Daniel would disembark.

When she saw the sailboat enter the marina, then lower the sails to slowly cruise its way to the slip, a thought crossed her mind. Did Daniel really love her? Or was this just a ploy to get her to agree to marry him?

She immediately pushed the ludicrous idea to the back of her mind. No man went to the lengths Daniel had to convince her that he loved her if he didn't mean it.

Watching him step off the boat, she lifted her long

skirt and ran the short distance to meet him under the balloon arch. As she gazed into his eyes, the love she saw shining in their navy depths stole her breath. "You really mean it, don't you?"

"I really do," he said, nodding. Wrapping his arms around her, he pulled her to him for a kiss that left them both gasping for breath. "I love you, Lily Kincaid."

The crowd behind them burst into applause.

As they walked past her mother on the way back up the pier, Lily stopped to give Elizabeth a hug. "You were right, Momma. He does love me."

Her mother nodded at she dabbed at her eyes with a lace-edged handkerchief. "I know, darling." Elizabeth hugged Daniel. "I'm so very happy for both of you."

Not to be outdone, Charlotte Addison kissed Lily's cheek. "Thank you for making my son more happy than I've ever seen him," she whispered. Turning to her son, she smiled. "You were right, Daniel. Equal in every way."

"Thank you, Charlotte," Daniel answered. "That means a lot."

"What did your mother mean by that?" Lily asked as they moved on through the crowd.

"I'll explain later." He grinned. "There's more to come. The surprise isn't over with just yet. "

"It isn't?" She couldn't imagine what he could possibly do to top the message on the sailboat.

When they reached Kara, he asked, "Is it here?"

"Right this way," her sister said, as she raised her hand to wave. A horse-drawn Victorian-style carriage immediately rolled up in front of them at her sister's signal. "We'll meet you back at the Beauchamp House."

Once she and Daniel were seated in the carriage and

it was slowly making its way down East Battery, Lily turned to kiss his cheek. "I can't believe you did all this for me."

"I had to, Lily," he said, putting his arm around her shoulders and tucking her to his side to shield her from the chill of the late-afternoon air. "I knew if I just told you that I love you, you wouldn't believe me."

She shook her head. "Probably not. You had me convinced that you didn't believe in love."

"I didn't." He kissed her forehead. "At least not until I asked a beautiful princess with long red hair and the prettiest blue eyes I've ever seen to dance with me at the Autumn Charity Ball. The moment I took her into my arms, I fell in love. I was just too stubborn to admit it."

Lowering his head, Daniel settled his lips over hers. There was such emotion, such love in his kiss that it brought tears to her eyes. Daniel did love her and she loved him with every fiber of her being.

When the carriage stopped in front of the mansion, her family and Charlotte were waiting for them and, escorting them in, Daniel led the way to the formal dining room. A huge cake with a prince-and-princess figurine on top sat in the middle of the long dining table. It had Congratulations, Lily and Daniel written in purple on the white icing.

"Congratulations?" Lily asked, looking around at her smiling family. "For what?"

Daniel had only professed his love. He hadn't proposed. Not really. His pragmatic suggestion that they get married a couple of weeks ago didn't count.

Before she realized what was happening, Daniel dropped to one knee and, in front of her family and his mother, took her hand in his. "Lily Kincaid, I love you more than life itself. Will you do me the honor of marrying me?"

Until that moment, she hadn't noticed the beautiful diamond solitaire he had poised to slip on the third finger of her left hand. "Y-yes!" One by one tears began to roll slowly down her cheeks. "I love you so much. Yes, I'll marry you, Daniel."

Sliding the white-gold ring into place, he rose to his feet and pulled her into his arms. "Do you want to tell everyone the rest of our news now?" he whispered close to her ear.

"They're all here. I think now would be a good time," she said.

"Lily and I have a little more news we'd like to share with you," Daniel said, smiling down at her.

"We're going to have a baby toward the end of summer," Lily said, gazing up at the man she loved.

A collective cheer went up from her family, and Lily was amazed to see her mother and Charlotte locked in a tearful hug. Both women may have already known about the pregnancy, but now they were able to celebrate freely the upcoming birth of their grandchild.

"I'm so happy for you about getting married and having a baby on the way," Kara said, hugging Lily. "Please tell me you'll let me plan your wedding and baby shower."

"I wouldn't think of having anyone else," Lily said honestly. "I can't believe the lengths you went to make today so perfect."

"Yes, thank you for everything, Kara," Daniel added, his expression grateful. "When I called you the other day to tell you what I had in mind, you took my idea and ran with it." He smiled. "Believe me, you outdid yourself. Today went above and beyond any of my expectations."

Kara looked extremely pleased. "I was glad to do it and I'm thrilled you liked the results." Turning to Lily, she advised, "When you decide on a date, let me know. It's never too early to start planning."

"We'll let you know as soon as we do," Lily promised.

Long after his mother and Lily's family left, Daniel sat with his arms around Lily on the new window seat in the cupola. "I love you, Lily," he said, kissing her temple. "More than you'll ever know."

Now that he had acknowledged his feelings for her, he couldn't seem to stop telling her. But he didn't think she minded. Each time he told her, the love he saw in her vivid blue eyes shined a little brighter.

"When do you want to get married?" she asked, leaning back against his chest as they gazed out at the star-studded night sky.

"As soon as possible," he said without hesitation.

Lily nodded. "I'll have to check with Kara on dates she has available."

"I was thinking that we might go ahead and get married right away and then have a big wedding sometime this fall after the baby is born," he said, hoping she was receptive to the idea.

She was silent for a moment and he thought he might have made her angry with his suggestion. "Actually, I like that idea," she finally said. "I think I would like to have a mid-October wedding—around the same time we met last year at the Autumn Charity Ball."

"Sounds good to me," he said, meaning it. "October is my lucky month."

She turned her head to look up over her shoulder at him. "Really? I wasn't aware you had one of those."

"I didn't until last year," he said, grinning. "When I met you and asked you to dance."

"Good answer, Addison." She kissed his chin. "Are you trying to get lucky again?"

He chuckled. "Not until morning, sweetheart. You've had a big day and I'm pretty sure when we go downstairs to the master suite, you're going to fall asleep the minute your head hits the pillow."

"You're probably right," she said, hiding a yawn behind her hand.

They both fell silent for some time, before she spoke again. "Thank you for giving me my dream."

Turning her in his arms, he shook his head as he gazed at the woman he loved more than life itself. "Your dad gave the princess her castle."

"That's true." Lily cupped his cheek with her soft hand. "But you gave me the prince I had been standing in the cupola waiting to see sail into Charleston Harbor. The man who will live with me in the castle and help me fill it with happy little princes and princesses." She kissed him. "I love you, Daniel Addison."

"And I love you, Lily Kincaid. For the rest of our lives."

* * * * *

*Turn the page for an exclusive short story
By* USA TODAY *bestselling author Day Leclaire.*

Then look for the next installment of
DYNASTIES: THE KINCAIDS,
WHAT HAPPENS IN CHARLESTON...
By USA TODAY *bestselling author Rachel Bailey*
Wherever Harlequin Books are sold.

The Kincaids: Jack and Nikki, Part 1

She emerged from cold, velvety blackness into a pool of firelight thrown from torches positioned strategically around the impeccably landscaped backyard and patio of the Colonel Samuel Beauchamp House. Even though she'd arrived late to the charity event, she didn't hurry. From his position on the second-floor balcony Jack Sinclair caught sight of her before anyone else in the gathering below. And he didn't think he'd ever seen anyone more beautiful.

"What am I offered for this fine bachelor?" the auctioneer called out, a hint of sarcasm underscoring his final two words. Clearly not a fan of his, Jack surmised. "Come on, folks. Remember, this is for charity."

The woman moved with the grace and power of a

goddess, hair as dark as a midnight sky falling from a center part to gently cup her shoulders. A wintry breeze gusted, lifting the feathered fringe across her brow and blowing it away from a classic, aristocratic face featuring high, elegant cheekbones and arching brows. Her gently curved chin spoke of a stubborn nature, while full, lush lips begged for a lover's kiss.

The goddess kept coming, moving through the crowd without breaking stride, her tall, lean shape encased in formfitting black wool, all she needed to hold Charleston's unusually temperate winter weather at bay. She paused beneath the balcony where he stood and tilted her head to stare up at him. Her gaze held a feminine challenge that aroused his most primitive desires, and even from a solid twenty feet away he could see that her eyes possessed all the glitter and brilliance of a flawless sapphire.

Jack looked…and he hungered.

"Someone? Anyone?" the auctioneer persisted. "One entire evening of fancy dining and dancing for the low, low price of fifty dollars. Do I hear twenty-five? Every penny goes to support Read and Write, promoting literacy in everyone from five to ninety-five."

His plea was met with a silence that roiled and seethed with each passing second, tumbling viciously through the men and women gathered below, all of whom smiled at the unmistakable message their silence sent. *You don't belong. You're not one of us. You have been tried, judged and found wanting.*

Grouped to one side stood his family. Fine. Not his family. They were the "Legitimates." The sons and daughters of his father's legally wedded-and-bedded wife, Elizabeth, while Jack was Reginald Kincaid's bastard son, forced to carry the name of his mother's late husband, Richard Sinclair, even though they didn't share a blood relationship. He allowed a brief, cold smile to cut through his carefully dispassionate expression. Hell, even his half brother, Alan Sinclair—another "Legitimate," though from the Sinclair side of his family—had aligned himself with the Kincaids. No surprise there.

Of course, the only reason Jack had been allowed to step foot on his half sister's property was because he sat on the board of Read and Write and had been talked into this ridiculous stunt long before the venue had been set. Otherwise, he was willing to bet Lily Kincaid would have barred him from attending. And now he'd pay the price. No one would bid on him and he'd be forced to suffer the public humiliation.

Well, screw 'em. Screw their fine, aristocratic backgrounds. Screw their hunger to put an upstart bastard in his place. Screw their cruelty. If it weren't for the children, he'd walk away and never look back. But he knew what harm illiteracy could cause. It was a war he believed in and would fight every day of his life, regardless of a little humiliation.

"Final call for bids," the auctioneer said, an edge of desperation to his voice. "Who will make an offer? Anyone? Twenty dollars? Ten dollars?"

"One thousand dollars!"

Those three words rang through the crowd. If it had been silent before, now that silence deepened, ringing with a shock so profound Jack could have heard the proverbial pin drop. As though acknowledging that fact, his goddess smiled. "But I expect value for my money," she called up to him. "Is dinner and dancing all you're offering?"

He allowed a brief grin to come and go. "What more would you like?"

"Anything?"

"Name it and it's yours."

Now, where the hell had that offer come from? Jack had been a businessman long enough to know better than to make such an unconditional proposal. He'd learned to look at every angle and all potential outcomes, to close every loophole and employ a ruthlessness that had earned him the nickname "the Bastard" in business, as well as birth. But it had only taken one blue-eyed, come-hither look from a face capable of making angels weep, and he'd offered the woman a loophole the size of Montana.

The murmur of voices rippled through the crowd, the sound slowly escalating with each passing second. Not that his goddess noticed. Her full attention remained fixed on him. Slowly, she smiled. Not a calculating look like so many of the women he'd known, but a warm, teasing expression that delighted in his offer.

"Then what I want is one wish to be fulfilled whenever and wherever I say," she informed him. "I think that's worth a thousand dollars."

Well, hell. "And then some."

"You made the offer." She shrugged. "I merely accepted your terms."

And with that, she turned on her heel and disappeared into the crowd, the shouted "Sold!" washing behind in her wake. He tracked her progress until the darkness swallowed her once again, darkness melting into darkness. The auctioneer gestured for him to surrender his place to the next bachelor in line. He didn't hesitate. He plunged through the open doorway into the salon off the master bedroom and threaded his way through the house.

He had a goddess to find.

Nikki could sense his approach, feel the punch that came from a man who exuded power both physically as well as through strength of personality. What in the world had she done? Not two hours after returning from an amazing two-week vacation, she'd hightailed it over to the bachelor auction she'd promised to attend before leaving for Aruba…and bid on a complete stranger. Worse, she'd flirted with him in front of half of the movers and shakers that dominated Charleston high society. No doubt her mother's phone would be ringing off the hook within the hour.

He came after her out of the darkness, a shaft of moonlight silvering his dark brown hair and catching in the unnerving robin's egg blue of his eyes. At six foot two he topped her by a solid five inches…or would if her boot heels didn't gift her with an extra few precious inches. She was more accustomed to looking men directly in the eye. Preferred it. But with this one, she needed to look up—up over a fabulous physique that began with powerful legs, a backside just rounded enough to give definition to his trousers, a tux jacket that emphasized mile-wide shoulders and finally his face. Tough. Ruthless. Shrewd. The entire package was mouthwatering and then some.

"Are you a cop?" The thoughtless question escaped before she could prevent it. Even though she'd learned long ago to think before speaking, sometimes her control slipped. Like now.

He stiffened, those powerful eyes narrowing. "No. Are you concerned you might need one?"

Uh-oh. Somehow she'd offended him. She dismissed his question with a careless shrug and attempted to backpedal. "I suppose my question didn't come out quite right."

"Then why don't you rephrase." It wasn't a question.

"You just have the look of a cop." She gestured toward his face. "You know, that 'I'll get my man no matter what it takes' sort of intensity. Plus, you were able to track me down. Not easy in the dark."

"It also wasn't hard. People looked at me, then looked in the direction you'd taken." He examined her in a focused way, as though attempting to dissect who and what she was. Still coplike and she should know, considering her father had worn the uniform. "I'm Jack, by the way."

"Nikki," she supplied, offering her hand.

He took it, swallowed it in a huge paw that made her look downright dainty in comparison, something not easy to do. His grip also filled her with an unexpected warmth, the hold almost protective. How strange. Ever since her father had died, she'd always been the protector of the family, the go-to person whenever an emergency cropped up or a difficult decision needed to be made. The strong one. And yet, she'd bet every last penny of the thousand dollars she'd just spent that Jack would do all that and more. For some reason, she found the thought deeply unsettling.

"I suppose we should exchange cell numbers in

order to set up our dinner," she suggested, tugging her hand free.

He released her and reached inside his tux jacket, removing a sleek, black PDA. "Not to mention the wish you managed to throw into the bargain. Clever of you."

"Mmm. A thousand dollars' worth of clever. Still," she added with a shrug, "I don't mind since I consider it money well spent. I'm a huge advocate of literacy."

"As am I."

Something in Jack's voice warned that it hit on a personal level. Interesting. Maybe something to pursue during their dinner date. Nikki exchanged numbers with him, adding him to her contacts list. They stood far too close, something she did her best to ignore though it proved an almost impossible challenge.

Heaven help her, but his scent was amazing, combining a quiet masculine fragrance with what she suspected he'd smell like fresh and naked from the shower. Authority exuded from him, an innate cloak of form and personality, intensely and overwhelmingly male. And she could feel the slow assault to her softer, more feminine defenses, the tremble of crumbling walls before the impending breach. She needed to find a way to reinforce those defenses, to hold herself at a safe distance. After all, hadn't she learned that powerful men weren't to be trusted? Of course she had. She'd learned that brutal fact in the most devastating way possible.

She spared Jack a swift look. As reluctant as she was to set them at odds with each other so early in their acquaintance, she didn't have any choice. She needed to protect herself first and foremost. And she knew just how to build a bulwark between them. One simple question was all it would take to drop it into place.

"Why wouldn't anyone bid on you?" she asked with seeming casualness.

He stepped back and she froze at the fierce expression in his eyes. She'd hoped to create some breathing room between them. She hadn't expected to stir such an intense reaction. "Don't you know?" he demanded softly.

"No."

His disbelieving gaze swept over her. She'd seen that sort of flat, penetrating look before. Her father had possessed it, along with the hard, cold cop eyes that went with it. So did his ex-partner, Charles McDonough, now a detective on the Charleston police force. Jack examined her inch by inch, appraising the cost of her clothing, the quality of the designer. Then he stripped her. Weighed her. Calculated her worth as a person, identified her background and education. Her intellect and personality. Her brand new tan, courtesy of her trip to Aruba.

"You're one of them," he said at last.

She didn't deny it. Couldn't. "My mother's family is." Her mouth curved to one side. "I guess you could say I straddle the line."

His intensity eased somewhat. "How?" he asked simply.

"My father's family all served in the military or law enforcement in one capacity or another. Blue-collar to a man, while mother's kin are old Southern aristocracy. It made for an…odd upbringing, to say the least."

To her surprise he actually returned her smile. "An upbringing we share."

She gestured in the direction of the charity auction, still ongoing, the sounds distant and muted from their position by the Beauchamp carriage house. "That's what they hold against you?" she asked, the question shaded with doubt. "You aren't part of Charleston aristocracy? That seems a little extreme, even for them."

"That's only one among many sins attributed to me, none of which need worry you."

"What should worry me?" she asked dryly.

The moon chose that moment to slip behind a bank of clouds, throwing his expression into shadow at the very instant she needed to see it the most. His voice issued from the darkness, want making it ripe and deep, sinking into her pores like a searing caress. "Only one thing."

Jack wrapped his fists around Nikki's soft lamb's wool collar and jerked her closer. Her body collided with his, pliant capitulating to unforgiving. Her walls trembled once again beneath the unexpected assault, breached by heat and need, and she teetered on the edge of yielding.

She knew what he intended, just as she knew she could escape if she struggled. But she didn't want to struggle. Curiosity filled her, a trait that had cursed womankind from the creation of Eve. It had been so long since she'd had a man's hands on her, known his touch. His possession. His kiss. She suspected Jack would excel at the art. There was only one way to find out for certain.

She lifted her face, allowed a shard of moonlight to splinter across her surrender. Without another word, he leaned in, took her mouth. Took her. She went under for the first count, swamped by a wave of desire higher and more powerful than she ever thought possible. His mouth felt firm against hers. In control. Oh, God...delicious! She came up for air just long enough to sigh out his name before the second wave slammed into her, sending her plummeting into desire again. Her lips parted and he swept inward, driving her insane with a tantalizing duel that filled her with a sharp, almost painful yearning. So long. So painfully long since a man had held her. Wanted her. Made her forget propriety and lessons learned.

A slight noise shattered the silence, penetrating the mist of passion that enclosed them, coming from somewhere between where they stood near the front doors of the carriage house and the courtyard. It almost had Nikki surfacing again. But at the last instant she went under for the third and final time, all too happy to drown in Jack's embrace.

"Hello?" came a woman's voice. "Who's there?"

It bothered Nikki to no end that she wasn't the one to terminate the kiss. Jack did, had the self-possession to pull back and regard her with a smile of masculine amusement. "I believe that's my cue to leave," he murmured.

A woman stepped into the intimate circle—one of the Kincaids, if Nikki wasn't mistaken. Her startled look flickered from Jack to Nikki and back again. Then her blue eyes narrowed in open displeasure.

"You have my number," he informed Nikki. "Call me when you're ready to pick up where we left off. Lily," he greeted the woman, tossing her a smile of open amusement—and possibly a hint of challenge—before melting into the darkness.

Dear God, what the hell had he been thinking, allowing lust to override common sense?

Jack worked his way around the crowd toward the front of Beauchamp House, his features set in a hard, ruthless expression that held all possible intruders at bay. And they would have approached, he knew it for a fact. Their fascination and curiosity, particularly in response to Nikki's outrageous bid, threatened to overcome their wariness. He refused to give them the opportunity, particularly after his reception at the charity auction...or lack thereof.

Of course, not everyone had been unwelcoming. His thoughts flashed to the woman who'd bid on him. Nikki. Now that he thought about it, he hadn't asked for her last name. What sort of fool did that make him? Ah, well. He had her phone number. So long as she wasn't a Kincaid—or affiliated with them—he didn't give a damn what her name was.

He did find one thing intriguing. Clearly, Nikki didn't recognize him, didn't associate him with the scandal that had broken early in January, following on the heels of his father's death—now ruled a murder. Didn't realize that he was Reginald Kincaid's bastard son.

Jack doubted it had even occurred to her to ask his full name, any more than he had hers, or chances were excellent she'd have made the connection. Would she still have bid on him if she'd known? When she found out the truth would she cancel their dinner date? Because guaranteed, someone would be all too happy to break the news, probably Lily.

He'd just have to deal with the possibility of her canceling if, or more likely when, it occurred. For some reason the knowledge that she'd follow the lead of the rest of Charleston's high society filled him with impotent fury, which didn't make the least sense. He'd known Nikki for less than an hour. Considering the craziness of the past month, he couldn't afford any distractions, particularly those of the female persuasion. Even so...

Man, she was gorgeous. Everything about her appealed, from the long-legged length of her, to the raven's wing sweep of hair, to the elegant features dominated by eyes jewel-blue bright. And then there was that kiss. He could still taste the delicate ripeness of her mouth. Still feel the lingering effects of the fragrant warmth of her body against his, the feminine curves that he'd have given just about anything to explore with a slow thoroughness that would end in only one way.

With the delicious Nikki in his bed.

Maybe he could handle one additional complication in his life. Dealing with the headaches—and opportunities—created by his inheritance of a forty-five-percent share of The Kincaid Group, in addition to the demands of his own business, Carolina Shipping, made for a very full plate. But maybe Nikki would offer a tantalizing dessert.

And everyone saved room for dessert, right?

"It's Nikki Thomas, isn't it?" the woman who'd interrupted Jack's kiss asked. Her gaze strayed in the direction Jack had taken, an odd expression flitting across her face.

Nikki nodded, vaguely recognizing the other woman from the various social functions they'd both attended. Recognizing, too, that she was a Kincaid. "That's right. You're Laurel's sister...Lily? Or is it Kara?" She offered

an apologetic smile. "Sorry. I know Laurel from work, but haven't quite gotten the rest of the family straight."

"I'm Lily. The youngest. Laurel is oldest, then Kara—short brown hair, not quite as curly as mine? You might not have met her since she doesn't work for The Kincaid Group. Then there's me." Amusement gleamed in her blue eyes. "Not to mention two brothers thrown into the mix at various points between, of course."

"RJ and Matthew. Yes, I run into them at work, as well."

"That's right." Lily spared another glance over her shoulder. Clearly, something about Jack's presence bothered her. "Are you a friend of Jack's?" she asked hesitantly.

"I met him for the first time tonight. Why?"

Shock replaced Lily's amusement. "Then, what in the world made you bid a thousand dollars for him?"

Okay. There was something going on here. Something Nikki hadn't quite gotten a handle on. "No one else seemed willing to and I felt sorry for the guy. So, tell me. Why was he getting the cold-shoulder treatment?"

Lily gave her an odd look. "You don't know?"

"Clearly not." A sense of unease filled her. "What? He's an ex-con? A gigolo? Swindles little old ladies out of their fortunes?"

"I wouldn't put any of those things past him," Lily stunned Nikki by admitting. "Though that's not what I have against him."

"Which is…?" Nikki prompted.

"I thought you worked for TKG."

"I do. I'm your family's corporate investigator."

"Then you must know about Jack, know he's in direct competition with our family's business. The rumors about him have been flying ever since my father died." Pain flashed across her face. "Was murdered," she corrected carefully.

Nikki froze. "Wait." Oh, God. She couldn't have made such a hideous mistake. Granted, she'd been in Aruba for the past two weeks, which had put her totally out of the loop. Still... Her heart rate kicked up a notch and a knot formed in the pit of her stomach. She moistened lips gone bone dry. "Are you saying that Jack, the Jack I just bid on is—"

Lily nodded. "Jack Sinclair. My father's illegitimate son."

* * * * *

PASSION

For a spicier, decidedly hotter read—
this is your destination for romance!

COMING NEXT MONTH
AVAILABLE FEBRUARY 14, 2012

#2137 TO KISS A KING
Kings of California
Maureen Child

#2138 WHAT HAPPENS IN CHARLESTON...
Dynasties: The Kincaids
Rachel Bailey

#2139 MORE THAN PERFECT
Billionaires and Babies
Day Leclaire

#2140 A COWBOY IN MANHATTAN
Colorado Cattle Barons
Barbara Dunlop

#2141 THE WAYWARD SON
The Master Vintners
Yvonne Lindsay

#2142 BED OF LIES
Paula Roe

Rhonda Nelson

SIZZLES WITH ANOTHER INSTALLMENT OF

When former ranger Jack Martin is assigned to provide security to Mariette Levine, a local pastry chef, he believes this will be an open-and-shut case. Yet the danger becomes all too real when Mariette is attacked. But things aren't always what they seem, and soon Jack's protective instincts demand he save the woman he is quickly falling for.

THE KEEPER

Available February 2012
wherever books are sold.

*Louisa Morgan loves being around children.
So when she has the opportunity to tutor bedridden Ellie,
she's determined to bring joy back into the motherless
girl's world. Can she also help Ellie's father open his
heart again? Read on for a sneak peek of*

THE COWBOY FATHER

by Linda Ford,
available February 2012 from Love Inspired Historical.

Why had Louisa thought she could do this job? A bubble of self-pity whispered she was totally useless, but Louisa ignored it. She wasn't useless. She could help Ellie if the child allowed it.

Emmet walked her out, waiting until they were out of earshot to speak. "I sense you and Ellie are not getting along."

"Ellie has lost her freedom. On top of that, everything is new. Familiar things are gone. Her only defense is to exert what little independence she has left. I believe she will soon tire of it and find there are more enjoyable ways to pass the time."

He looked doubtful. Louisa feared he would tell her not to return. But after several seconds' consideration, he sighed heavily. "You're right about one thing. She's lost everything. She can hardly be blamed for feeling out of sorts."

"She hasn't lost everything, though." Her words were quiet, coming from a place full of certainty that Emmet was more than enough for this child. "She has you."

"She'll always have me. As long as I live." He clenched his fists. "And I fully intend to raise her in such a way that even if something happened to me, she would never feel like I was gone. I'd be in her thoughts and in her actions every day."

Peace filled Louisa. "Exactly what my father did."

Their gazes connected, forged a single thought about fathers and daughters…how each needed the other. How sweet the relationship was.

Louisa tipped her head away first. "I'll see you tomorrow."

Emmet nodded. "Until tomorrow then."

She climbed behind the wheel of their automobile and turned toward home. She admired Emmet's devotion to his child. It reminded her of the love her own father had lavished on Louisa and her sisters. Louisa smiled as fond memories of her father filled her thoughts. Ellie was a fortunate child to know such love.

Louisa understands what both father and daughter are going through. Will her compassion help them heal—and form a new family? Find out in
THE COWBOY FATHER
by Linda Ford, available February 14, 2012.

Love Inspired Books celebrates 15 years of inspirational romance in 2012! February puts the spotlight on Love Inspired Historical, with each book celebrating family and the special place it has in our hearts. Be sure to pick up all four Love Inspired Historical stories, available February 14, wherever books are sold.

USA TODAY bestselling author

Sarah Morgan

brings readers another enchanting story

ONCE A FERRARA WIFE...

When Laurel Ferrara is summoned back to Sicily
by her estranged husband, billionaire
Cristiano Ferrara, Laurel knows things are about
to heat up. And Cristiano's power is a potent
reminder of his Sicilian dynasty's unbreakable rule:
once a Ferrara wife, always a Ferrara wife....

Sparks fly this February